Naguib Mahfouz (1911–2006) was Egypt's most eminent writer. Over a career that lasted more than five decades, he wrote thirty-four novels, thirteen short story anthologies, numerous plays and thirty screenplays. His works range from re-imaginings of ancient myths to subtle commentaries on contemporary Egyptian politics and culture. A writer of incredible discipline, every day he wrote for one hour, smoked three cigarettes and walked by the Nile. In 1994, he was stabbed in the neck by religious extremists and was seriously wounded. The injury caused nerve damage that partly paralysed his right hand, preventing him from writing. Of his many novels, his most famous in English translation is *The Cairo Trilogy*, consisting of *Palace Walk*, *Palace of Desire* and *Sugar Street*. Other notable works include *Children of the Alley*, *The Thief and The Dogs* and *Autumn Quail*. Naguib Mahfouz received the Nobel Prize in Literature in 1988, the first writer in Arabic to do so.

Praise for Naguib Mahfouz

'The Arab world's foremost novelist ... Arabic has a rich tradition in poetry, but the novel was not a strong art form until Mahfouz made it accessible.' *New York Times*

'[Mahfouz] populated his works with a cast of memorably strong urban characters. ... The result was a body of work that bore comparison with Balzac and Dickens. Mahfouz introduced his audience to a new way of seeing.' *The Economist*

'The world of Naguib Mahfouz is vast and extremely rich. He spans the various changes in the reality, dreams and

aspirations of his nation. Although his world is mainly Cairo and the old quarter of Gamaliya in which he spent his childhood, he made the urban scene an elaborate and highly significant metaphor of the national condition.'
Independent

'Egypt's greatest living writer ... one of the world's most humane literary figures. Like Zola, Mahfouz chronicled the lives of the most ordinary of his countrymen ... Like Dostoyevsky, he set most of his novels in one beloved city – Cairo, in his case. Like his elders Taha Husayn and Tawfiq al-Hakim, he took on the role of national storyteller.' *The Nation*

'Mahfouz's work is freshly nuanced and hauntingly lyrical. The Nobel Prize acknowledges the universal significance of [his] fiction.' *Los Angeles Times*

'Mahfouz's scope is vast and his concerns are not only still evident today, but crucial.' *The Scotsman*

Praise for The Cairo Trilogy

'Luminous ... All the magic, mystery and suffering of Egypt in the 1920s are conveyed on a human scale.' *New York Times Book Review*

'It is Mahfouz's wonderful ability to delineate human beings from their outer appearances which gives *Palace Walk* its universal appeal. I shall read it again and again.' *The Guardian*

'A masterpiece.' *The Times*

'Teeming with life and contention ... it promises riches.'
Independent

'Naguib Mahfouz's *Cairo Trilogy* puts all contemporary writers in the shade. He is the Arab Tolstoy.' Simon Sebag Montefiore

'The alleys, the houses, the palaces and mosques and the people who live among them are evoked as vividly as the streets of London were conjured up by Dickens.' *Newsweek*

'An engrossing work, whose author can take his place alongside any European master you care to name' *Sunday Times*

'A magnificent, Tolstoyan saga ... unmissable.' *Cosmopolitan*

'*The Cairo Trilogy* extends our knowledge of life; it also confirms it.' *Boston Globe*

'A grand novel of ideas ... a marvellous read.' *Washington Post*

'*Sugar Street* is a marvellous novel, with many messages, open and concealed, for those who will be instructed.' *TLS*

'A masterful kaleidoscope of emotions, ideas and perspective.' *Newsday*

'Mahfouz's genius is not just that he shows us Egyptian colonial society in all its complexity; it is that he makes us look through the vision of his vivid characters and see people and ideas that no longer seem alien.' *Philadelphia Inquirer*

Naguib Mahfouz

THE QUARTER

Translated from Arabic by Roger Allen

SAQI

Saqi Books
26 Westbourne Grove
London W2 5RH
www.saqibooks.com

Published 2019 by Saqi Books
2

First published in Arabic by Dar al Saqi in 2018

Printed and bound by Clays Ltd, Elcograf S.p.A

A full CIP record for this book is available from the British Library

ISBN 978 0 86356 375 1
eISBN 978 0 86356 385 0

CONTENTS

FOREWORD

By Elif Shafak

I first read the works of Naguib Mahfouz in Istanbul in Turkish. Back then, as a university student, I used to frequent a second-hand bookshop – a low-ceilinged, musty-smelling place with plank floors, just a stone's throw from the Grand Bazaar.

The owner of the bookshop – a sour-tempered, middle-aged man with thick glasses and a haircut that had never been popular in any era – genuinely loved books and equally disliked human beings. At times he would randomly pick a customer and quiz him or her on their knowledge of literature, history, science or philosophy. I had seen him scold people before, and though I had never witnessed it myself, urban legend held that he refused to sell books to customers who failed his tests. No doubt there were many other bookshops in the city where you didn't have to inhale dust or risk bumping your head on the door frames, and where you could choose books without being grilled by the owner. Yet I kept returning to this place. Getting the bookseller's seal of approval felt like a rite of passage, an unspoken challenge. Young and vain as I was, I secretly wanted him to question me on French, English or Russian novels in translation, which I believed were my 'strong point'. But on this rainy day in late autumn, he looked at me and asked, 'So, have you read Mahfouz?'

I froze. I had no idea who he was talking about. Slowly, I shook my head.

The bookseller said nothing, though his disappointment was visible. When I finished perusing and walked to the till, ready to pay for the books I had selected, he turned towards me with a frown. For a moment I feared he was going to kick me out of the shop. Instead, he grabbed a book from the shelf behind him and pushed it into my hands. Then he said, loud and clear: 'Read him!'

The book that the grumpy bookseller in Istanbul sold me on that day was *Midaq Alley*. For a while, I postponed reading it. Then, about two months later, I started the book, not knowing what to expect. Inside, I found a rich world that was at once familiar and magical, well-founded and elusive. The stories of the people of the alley – families, street vendors, poets, matchmakers, barbers, beggars and others – were so deftly told that I felt as though I knew them, each as the individuals they are. Istanbul, too, was full of such streets and neighbourhoods unable to keep up with the bewildering changes surrounding them, and it remained both isolated and central, both inside the city and on its periphery. By delving into this world with a sharp mind and compassionate heart, Mahfouz had shown me the extraordinary within the ordinary, the invisible within the visible, and the many layers underneath the surface. His writing, just like Cairo itself, pulsed with life and a quiet strength.

Mahfouz's Cairo was a fluid world. Nothing seemed permanently settled; nothing felt solid. As a nomad I was familiar with that feeling, and suddenly I found myself looking for more Mahfouz books to read.

And here was the odd part. Mahfouz was not well translated into other languages in the region for a long time. It was only after he received the Nobel Prize in Literature – the first author writing in Arabic to do so – that more of his oeuvre crossed national and ethnic borders. It troubled me back then, and still does, that in the Middle East we do not follow each other's writers and poets as well as we should.

Over the years I continued reading Mahfouz, mostly in English. He was a political writer. He knew that novelists from turbulent lands did not have the luxury of being non-political. I also read his interviews with interest. In these interviews there were moments when I did not agree with his views, which at times could be nationalistic, but I always respected his storytelling.

Many of his books were banned in Arab countries, in the very language he breathed in. This must have hurt him deeply. Mahfouz knew first-hand how painful it is to carve out a personal space of artistic freedom in lands without democracy and without freedom of speech. Significantly, he was among the literary figures who supported Salman Rushdie's right to write after a deadly *fatwa* was issued against the author. It is noteworthy that Mahfouz did this at a time and in a country where it wasn't easy for him to do so – although he later also made negative comments about Rushdie's novel, which he said he hadn't read.

In 1994, Mahfouz was stabbed by an extremist, who accused him of being 'an infidel'. The year before, in Turkey, Aziz Nesin, a prominent writer and satirist, who had announced his decision to publish *The Satanic Verses* in Turkish in defence of freedom of speech, was attacked by a mob of fundamentalists in the Anatolian town of Sivas, where he happened to be for a cultural festival. His hotel was set on fire and thirty-five people were killed – most of them were poets, writers, musicians and dancers. Once again in human history, fanatics targeted art and literature, words and notes, and destroyed innocent lives.

Mahfouz thankfully survived the attack in Cairo. Always a prolific writer, the physical damage and the constant pain he suffered afterwards considerably slowed him down. This, too, must have saddened him.

Throughout his entire literary journey, Naguib Mahfouz produced stories, novels, plays, scripts, experimenting with forms. One thing remained constant: his unwavering love for Cairo and its people. This city had made him who he was and in return, he re-created Cairo on the page. It is this existential challenge that strikes me most deeply perhaps. Mahfouz clearly yearned for freedom and autonomy, but he also had a remarkable loyalty towards and a longing for the motherland that denied him these basic rights.

I was excited when I learned the news that eighteen previously unknown stories by Naguib Mahfouz had been recently discovered among his old papers.

Irrational as it may be, there is a part of me that thinks he must be very happy. I imagine him caressing this new book while smoking a slim cigarette, with a cup of strong Turkish coffee by his side. I imagine him with a smile on his face, not a tired one, but the hopeful smile of the young novelist he once was.

One of the stories in this beautiful new collection ends with a striking dialogue: 'I've enough misery to deal with', says one of the characters, to which the other responds: 'So have I. Each of us needs the other.' Writers and readers from countries that have seen enough misery, injustice and sadness need each other, just like that.

INTRODUCTION

By Roger Allen

The discovery of a cache of eighteen previously unknown narratives by a Nobel Laureate in Literature is clearly a significant event. In the specific case of Naguib Mahfouz, the Egyptian Nobel Laureate for 1988, that is particularly the case in view of his central position in the development of modern Arabic fiction, and his constant and vigorous participation in Egyptian social and political life through both his journalistic and fictional writings.

What certainly enhances our interest in this collection are the circumstances surrounding their discovery in 2018, almost twelve years after the author's death. It appears that the Egyptian journalist Mohamed Shoair (whom I originally met in Cairo in the 1990s and with whom I have recently been in touch) has been in the process of writing a book about Mahfouz's most controversial work – the novel, *Awlad*

Haratina (*Children of the Alley*), originally published as a series of articles in the Cairene newspaper *Al-Ahram* in 1959. As part of Shoair's research, he was in contact with Mahfouz's daughter, Umm Kulthoum. He tells us that the manuscript of these narratives was found in a drawer with a note attached stating, 'To be published in 1994.' That particular year turned out to be a momentous one in Mahfouz's life and career. On 13 October, the anniversary of the announcement of his Nobel award in Stockholm in 1988, he was stabbed in the neck outside his flat in Dokki, a Cairo suburb, in an attempt to kill him. The prompt for this assassination attempt came from a *fatwa* (legal opinion) that had been issued by a radical Egyptian Muslim cleric, Omar Abdel-Rahman, the so-called 'blind sheikh' and leader of Al-Jama'a al-Islamiyya who had condemned Mahfouz for not declaring Salman Rushdie's *Satanic Verses* to be heretical, and for Mahfouz's earlier controversial work, *Awlad Haratina*. This traumatic event was to have a profound effect on Mahfouz (not least because a severed nerve in his neck now prevented him from actually using his writing hand). This mention of 1994 inevitably raises questions about the circumstances surrounding the composition of these eighteen narratives. Before examining the implications that can be drawn from the texts themselves, I will first discuss the precedents for these narratives in order to attempt to place them into the broader context of Mahfouz's total oeuvre.

The 'complete works' of Naguib Mahfouz had been published on a regular basis over the sixty-plus years of his career (almost all of them by Maktabat Misr, the publishing house of Mahfouz's longtime friend and associate, Abd al-Hamid Jawdat al-Sahhar, himself a novelist). A complete set of those works in English translation has now been published by the American University in Cairo Press. That said, diligent researchers have, from time to time, uncovered references to manuscripts of works, both published and unpublished, and Mahfouz himself admitted that he was never particularly concerned about the fate (and preservation) of the original manuscripts of his fictional creations. One anecdote will suffice: Mahfouz noted that, when, after five years of research, he completed the over 1,500-page manuscript of his famous *Cairo Trilogy* and took it to al-Sahhar's office in April 1952 (in other words, immediately prior to the Egyptian Revolution of July that year), the publisher – not unreasonably – balked at its size. Mahfouz left the office without the only copy of his manuscript. Fortunately for world literature, al-Sahhar retained the manuscript and went on to publish the work in three volumes in 1956 and 1957.

Thus, the finding of the manuscript of these eighteen narratives may not be an unprecedented discovery of previously unpublished Mahfouz texts, but something that may indeed stretch all the way back to the process of selecting stories for inclusion in his very first collection, *Hams al-junun* (*The Whisper of Madness*, 1938).

Into what historical and generic contexts can these narratives be plausibly inserted? Having read the texts and translated them into English, I have concluded that the central theme around which such questions can be most effectively addressed is that of the *hara* (quarter). Mahfouz's earliest writings in the 1930s were philosophical essays (reflecting his academic interests at the time) and short stories, and his first three novels (published 1939–42) reflect his lifelong interest in ancient Egypt (stimulated by weekly visits to the Egyptian Museum that he undertook with his mother – he being the youngest child of the family by well over a decade). However, political developments in Egypt during the 1930s and into the 1940s led him in an entirely new direction, a development that was clearly stimulated by his ongoing readings of European fictional works (based, we learn, on the listing of representative works to be found as an appendix to John Drinkwater's *The Outline of Literature*, 1923–24). It was in the 1940s that he began writing his so-called 'quarter novels,' the titles of at least two of which – *Khan al-Khalili* (1945?) and *Zuqaq al-Midaqq* (1947) – are very specific as to their location in the older quarters of Cairo. Following his Nobel award in 1988, Mahfouz took part in a film in which, along with his close friend, the novelist Gamal al-Ghitani, he returned to his childhood haunts. His lingering affection for those sites, with their lengthy histories, unique atmosphere and denizens (including, as he notes, the *futuwwat*, thug gangs), is continuingly reflected in his writings. However, his desire in the novels up to and including *The Cairo Trilogy* to reflect in detail the often-brutal realities of life in those quarters during the pre-revolutionary decades underwent a transformation after the 1952 revolution. After a significant pause in Mahfouz's fictional writing, the publication of *Awlad Haratina* in 1959 (first published in English as *Children of Gebelawi*, 1981) sees his fictional depictions of the *hara* emerge in an entirely new light.

The first episode of the series of articles, *Awlad Haratina*, appeared in the Cairene newspaper *Al-Ahram* in September 1959. Bearing in mind the instantaneous success that the volumes of Mahfouz's *Trilogy*, published just two years earlier, had enjoyed, it is not a little surprising that there was no announcement and no fanfare; the article simply begins with the title and the name of its author, Naguib Mahfouz. That said, it did not take long for readers to read between the lines and discover that this particular *hara* has its own maximally symbolic connotations, as the figure of Adham carefully replicates incidents in the life of the Biblical Adam, culminating in his expulsion from Eden. The quarter in the title of *Awlad Haratina*, it emerges, is portrayed by the novel's narrator, basing his narrative on the accounts of traditional bards, as the residence of successive generations of humans. Periods dominated by the benign influence of religious leaders (figures representing Moses, Jesus, Muhammad and 'Scientia') are interspersed with depictions of the violence of the quarter's gangs and against the continuing presence outside the quarter of the house of the mysterious figure of Jabalawi, who had originally ejected Adham for his disobedience.

The symbolic resonance of this continuing weekly

series did not escape the notice of Al-Azhar, the major institution of Muslim Sunni scholarship and learning in Cairo, who vigorously objected to its continuing publication. Despite their protests, the editor of *Al-Ahram*, Muhammad Hasanayn Haykal, refused to stop publication. However, when the series was completed (and its original version is still available on the archived pages of the newspaper), Mahfouz agreed with the authorities of Al-Azhar that it would never be published in book form in Egypt during his lifetime. However, in 1967 a book version of *Awlad Haratina* was published in Beirut, without Mahfouz's knowledge or permission.

I provide these details here because the institution of the *hara*, used in this highly symbolic fashion, was to become a frequent resort for Mahfouz in his subsequently published works, and, I would add, is clearly present in this new collection of eighteen narratives. It was in the 1970s, after a decade in which Mahfouz had produced an amazing number of fictional works – novels and short stories – characterised by an increasingly allusive and economical style, that he returned to the *hara* as a particular locus for his fictions. While *Hikayat Haratina* (1975; *Fountain and Tomb*, 1988), for example – with its seventy-eight tales set in

1920s Cairo and its concern for the lives of its quarter's inhabitants in a time of profound change, constitutes a clear precedent to the spatial context of these recently discovered narratives, it is Mahfouz's *Asda' al-Sira al-Dhatiyya* (1994; *Echoes of an Autobiography*, 1997) that, for a number of reasons, can be seen as having a direct relationship with them. Like *Awlad Haratina, Asda' al-Sira al-Dhatiyya* was first published in serialised form in *Al-Ahram*: 211 short narratives that appeared in the Friday edition of the newspaper between February and April 1994. The appearance of this lengthy series of articles, published initially during what was to prove to be a very significant time period – just a few months before Mahfouz was viciously attacked, and the addition of a note to the manuscript of these newly discovered narratives, stating 'To be published in 1994', lend a considerable significance to the apparent temporal juxtaposition of the two sets of texts and to the questions that I have raised above about both the timing and generic purpose of this new set.

Briefly stated, *Asda' al-Sira al-Dhatiyya* consists of a large collection of short, numbered texts which can be conveniently divided into two: in the first part, a narrator reminisces about days of yore and recalls incidents in his life and people whom he knew; in the second part (beginning with text no. 112) the reader is introduced to the figure of Sheikh Abd Rabbih al-Ta'ih (servant of his Lord, the wanderer), who dispenses homiletic wisdom to his listeners – for example, 'the only thing more stupid than a stupid believer is a stupid infidel,' and 'the most powerful people of all are those who forgive.'

In the eighteen texts collected in this volume, we are again dealing with a series of short narratives, each with its own title. The *hara* is the location of all the differently titled segments, but, as is the case with the other works that I have just mentioned, that location also assumes a broader and more symbolic function as the site of a sample of human society, with all its foibles, conflicts, relationships, triumphs and defeats. Two key figures have varying roles to play in each of the narratives: the first is the *shaykh al-hara*, the administrative head of the quarter; the second is the imam, the religious figure who supervises the local *zawiya*, a combination of a mosque, Qur'an school and fountain, and serves as a regular counsellor to the *shaykh al-hara*. In these narratives the two authority figures find themselves constantly at the centre of whatever actions are provoked by the quarter's inhabitants, whether they reside there or, as happens in some of the narratives, have returned after prolonged absences. Apart from the quarter and its centrally located mosque, there is one other location that is the focus of several of the narratives, the *qabw* near the old fort, which I have translated as 'cellar'. The people who either reside there or come to visit have an encounter with the unseen and unknown, a clear reflection of another of Mahfouz's ongoing interests throughout his career, that of Sufism and its frequent invocation of the twin concepts of *al-zahir* (the evident) and *al-batin* (the interior, hidden). In these narratives, those who have such encounters inside the cellar emerge from the experience with their perspectives changed, often requiring and provoking a confrontation with the authority figures in the quarter. These narratives then, like the others that we have discussed above, reveal the continuing craft of an author who uses a community and location of limited dimensions as a symbol to point to issues of more universal significance.

In talking about Mahfouz's techniques earlier, I alluded to his clear move to a more allusive and economical style, one that becomes even more so in his work of the 1990s. Mahfouz was fully conscious of the changes that he was undertaking. In a telephone conversation with me in 1971, he specifically drew my attention to a completely new mode of writing, as he termed it, that he was adopting for his series of vignettes, *Al-Maraya*. Unlike the 'quarter novels' of the 1940s, there is minimal description of place in these eighteen narratives; one would be hard pressed to use them as a basis for drawing a map of this particular 'quarter'. The reader is taken straight into the core of the narrative, with no preliminaries and few, if any, of the conventions of a genre such as the short story. Conversations, often involving confrontations and challenges to traditional norms, are plentiful, as inhabitants find themselves having to deal with unfamiliar situations and to resolve familial and social problems that fate and the forces of the unseen have thrown in their path.

While I have previously translated five of Mahfouz's novels and a collection of his short stories (up to 1970), it has proved a pleasant challenge for me to render into English the style and structure of the later Mahfouz reflected in these eighteen narratives. The decisions necessarily involved in that process of translation have led me inexorably to the conclusion that this recently discovered manuscript is a reflection of his later creative expressions involving the symbolic function of the *hara* rather than earlier phases in his long career as a writer. In the end, however, we are left with an unanswered (and probably unanswerable) question: since these eighteen narratives show a distinct unity of location, purpose and style, are they a complete work or merely part of what was to be a larger project that was begun but never completed? It is perhaps only appropriate that we are left with a mystery. Meanwhile, we are without a doubt grateful for this unexpected gift.

THE QUARTER

THE OVEN

The disaster had happened. Ayousha had run off with Zeinhum, the baker's boy. When the news broke, fragments scattered all over the quarter. Down every alleyway, at least one good heart expressed disbelief.

'God help us all! What a disaster for you, Amm Jumaa, you are a good man!'

The Amm Jumaa in question was Ayousha's father. Head of the family, he was the father of five strapping lads. Ayousha, his only daughter, was now fated to knock him off his pedestal of decency and respect.

It was only after the scandal blew up that anyone had anything to say about her. She was said to be beautiful and charming. Umm Radi, who sold spice-paste, declared:

'She's beautiful; there's no denying that. But she's too bold. Glances from those flashing eyes of hers go straight into the heart of the person she's talking to, so they forget what they're talking about.'

Amm Jumaa and his sons were devastated and simply stared at the ground. At first, they were so angry that they took to spreading out across the quarter, searching and listening for information. But it was fruitless.

'Mistakes can lead a person to commit crime,' the Head of the Quarter eventually told Amm Jumaa. 'He's lost whatever happens.'

Amm Jumaa kept a grip on himself on account of his sons.

'Just tell yourselves your sister's dead,' he told them. 'God will have mercy on her. Leave everything else to Him.'

Everyone put the story together as they saw fit, but it was predictable enough. The girl had met and fallen in love with the boy as he took the dough to the oven and brought home the bread. It would never be possible for the baker's son to ask for the hand of the daughter of a rich cloth-merchant; the two lovers had decided to run away. Ayousha collected her own jewellery and as much of her mother's as she could find, and they fled. The only conceivable conclusion to the story was that they would get married, wherever they were.

That was the end of the story of Ayousha and

Zeinhum. It took a very long time for the wound in Amm Jumaa's family to heal. They went back to their normal lives but suffered the usual downward spiral. The merchant went bankrupt and made plans to sell his house.

In the very depths of his misery, a messenger he did not recognise arrived with the money he needed.

'This money has been sent by your daughter, Ayousha,' the man said. 'Divine will has decreed that it is her husband, Zeinhum, who brings it to you.'

The man's son-in-law informed him that his wife had sold the jewellery she had taken and used it to open a bakery for him. After some hard times, they were now doing well.

'Do you see?' the Head of the Quarter told the mosque Imam. 'The girl's come back at just the right moment. You have no need to forgive her sin.'

YOUR LOT IN LIFE

We do not know precisely when the phenomenon began to occur. All those who witnessed it have their own version. Time lost its order. Here is what Amm Hifni, the water-seller, had to say:

'I went to the pastry-seller to buy some honey cakes with extra vegetable fat. He took a roll of dough, flattened it with a rolling pin and smoothed it with the palm of his hand. But just then he stopped what he was doing and burst into tears. I was stunned. I asked him what the matter was and what I could do to help. But he just kept on crying, holding out his hands, wringing them and sobbing again. People gathered in front of his shop until his family arrived and took him home, still crying.'

A woman who sells pickled vegetables said:

'Sitt Umm Ali came to my stall with a bowl to fill with pickled vegetables. At one moment she was pointing to the cucumbers and falafel, but then she suddenly stopped and her expression froze. She began weeping violently, and, as time went on, it only grew more intense and abundant. I was paralysed from head to toe; I worried I had done something to upset her. People gathered round, and her husband hurried over from his shop and took her home. Everyone looked at each other in shock and amazement.'

The stories kept multiplying and becoming more elaborate. There were many victims, both men and women. When the news reached the Head of the Quarter, he was irate.

'You people never stop inventing heresies and lies,' he said.

However, when he saw a guard break down in tears, he soon stopped blaming people and jumping to conclusions.

'So here's a new disaster in our quarter,' he told the mosque Imam. 'It never has its fill when it comes to generating disasters.'

'People cure the condition with hot baths and cold drinks,' the Imam responded.

Umm Haniyya, the bath-attendant, was close by.

'The only cure for it,' she interrupted, 'is a *zar* exorcism.'

'Are demons involved in this condition?' the Imam asked.

'No one ever cries for no reason,' she said. 'The only exception is if someone is touched by demons; in which case, the demon will only leave him if there's a *zar*.'

'I'm not prepared to accept,' said the Head of the Quarter emphatically, 'that the entire quarter is touched. However, I'll raise the matter with the Health Inspector.'

He duly went to see His Excellency the Inspector and told him the whole story.

'You're not separating reality from illusion,' was the Inspector's comment.

The Head of the Quarter then swore that he had seen the tears for himself; every house was affected. The next morning, the Inspector visited the quarter, accompanied by a guard and a nurse. The people rushed over:

'Help us, Your Excellency!' they all shouted.

He stared at them in fury, but his anger turned to amazement when he saw men and women weeping.

'Is there anything new about your way of life,' he asked the Head of the Quarter, 'that might explain this?'

'No, sir, absolutely nothing new. Our life is the way it is, with all its joys and sorrows.'

The Inspector went from house to house. He toured the entire quarter from one end to the other. He left no shop, café, fountain, Qur'an school or animal trough uninspected; he checked donkeys and mules and stared long and hard at the walls of the old fort and the cellar. He sat down in the Head of the Quarter's house, exhausted, and gazed off into the distance. Just then, Umm Haniyya's voice rose from the crowd that had gathered in front of the shop:

'The *zar* ritual!' she yelled. 'That's the only cure, Your Excellency.'

'Shut up, woman!' the Head of the Quarter yelled back angrily.

The Head of the Quarter expected the Inspector to say something, but he remained silent. He seemed more and more tired. Eventually the Head of the Quarter decided that the Inspector was about to collapse.

Master Hassan, the musician who owned the local cabaret, noticed the same thing. He suggested to the Head of the Quarter that he take the Inspector to his house to relax by the fountain. He would prepare him a cold drink and arrange some fresh flowers. To save them all from any further complications, the Head of the Quarter readily accepted the offer.

So the Inspector went to the musician's home. People began talking about their tragedies again.

'I'll bet you the Inspector will start weeping,' said one man.

'He's a human being,' the Head of the Quarter responded angrily. 'Everyone's susceptible to contagion.'

However, what emerged from the musician's house was the sounds of a pulsating rhythm, drumbeats and clapping. Someone looked out from the house facing the musician's home.

'He's dancing!' the man shouted. 'And what a dance it is!'

He heard the voice singing:

'Your lot in life is bound to find you …'

It seems he kept on dancing and singing.

People now thronged from every quarter and responded to the musician's poem.

All of a sudden, the people who were weeping stopped.

They all dissolved into laughter.

PURSUIT

Zakiyya came back to the quarter after a year away, with a nursing baby in her arms. No one had realised she had left or that she had come back. She still looked skinny and pale; indeed, she was barely there. The blush of beauty on her face had faded, leaving only traces of a long-departed youth. She kept looking at the three houses she had worked in as a servant, after the death of her mother Sukaina, the washer-woman. Eventually she stared hard at the last house, in the direction of the cellar. This was the home of Boss Uthman, who sold canes and umbrellas.

Zakiyya was so poor she could not afford to waste any time. She therefore decided to work as an unofficial vendor of children's sweets, such as Turkish delight and sugared caraway seeds. In one hand she would hold a basket full of halva squares and in the other she clutched her baby. She began to move from place to place, hawking her halva, but it seemed she was making a special point of standing in front of Boss Uthman's shop. She made sure that he could hear her voice or see her in person. He could not ignore her forever. When the place was empty, he saw his chance and signalled to her. When she came over, they exchanged looks, hers strong and steady, his deceptive.

'How are you, Zakiyya?' he asked.

'Praise be to God, in any event,' she responded gruffly.

'Do you need anything?'

'God is the great provider,' she replied boldly, 'but this baby needs his due, as decreed by God.'

'That's a long statement with no meaning. Just say that you're in need.'

'I said just what I mean,' she retorted angrily, 'and you in particular should understand.'

'I don't understand anything!' he shouted nervously. 'Get away from me. This is the reward for someone who takes pity on the undeserving.'

He disappeared inside, quivering with anger. She resumed her trade around the shop or nearby, never wavering from her plan. Hour after hour, she would be there, patient and determined. Meanwhile, he was shaking with fury, beset by all kinds of bloody dreams.

'Woe is me!' he said to himself as he felt the tension

build in his very soul, 'I can't concentrate on my work.'

He started to loathe his life, both in the shop and at home, sensing that he and his family were being manipulated by a demon.

'If you keep this up,' he whispered to her one day, on his way home, 'no one's going to find your corpse.'

She was not afraid, nor did she withdraw. Instead she was content to play with her baby. Boss Uthman could not stand it anymore, watching the world, and the woman carrying her baby, hovering around his shop. He took his friend, the Head of the Quarter, aside and shared his worries with him.

'What really scares me,' he finished by saying, 'is that she's going to create a scandal out of nothing.'

The Head of the Quarter stared at him long and hard but did not express any doubts about what he had been told.

'If the woman weren't making false claims,' he told Uthman, 'I would advise you to swallow your pride and get back to doing the work God has ordained for you.'

'But she is making false claims,' Uthman replied in a broken voice.

'She can still embroil you in a scandal, and people will believe her.'

'But you wouldn't let that happen.'

'I'll work on getting her to leave the quarter,' said the Head of the Quarter, after a moment's reflection. 'She'll get a monthly stipend, which we'll consider charity. That will be the best solution all round.'

'I'll fulfill the obligation you suggest,' sighed Boss Uthman.

Next day the Head of the Quarter summoned Zakiyya.

'I have a happy solution for you,' he said.

He told her about the agreement that had been reached.

'You'll be living in a respectable household,' he told her, 'and I'll commend you to your new head of quarter.'

Silence stretched between them, a silence full of thoughts and obscure emotions. The Head of the Quarter realised that he was not getting the response he had hoped for.

'Did you hear what I said?' he asked her.

'I heard what you said, Head of the Quarter,' she replied, her neck rigid. 'But I'm not leaving.'

'You're crazy!' The Head of the Quarter was angry. 'That's obvious.'

'This baby is his child,' she said. 'I won't accept that kind of charity.'

'What are you planning to do?'

'To keep the baby where he can see it, so he'll always remember his crime.'

Zakiyya kept up her daily routine, selling halva, taking care of the baby, and hovering in the vicinity of the shop. Boss Uthman sank further and further into suppressed misery. His anger only grew darker and more intense, and, maybe for the first time in his life, he considered murder.

But then something else occurred to him, and, right in the middle of the working day, at his wits' end, he went to see the Head of the Quarter.

'I'll marry her and acknowledge the baby,' he shouted, grabbing the Head of the Quarter's hand as though begging for help. 'We'll have to live in another quarter.'

The Head of the Quarter's reply was crystal clear:

'That woman will never give ground on a single thing.'

SON OF THE QUARTER

From as far back as anyone could remember he had been called 'Son of the Quarter.' He had no known father or mother. The territory of the quarter was his turf, the cellar was his dormitory, and offering minor services was his trade and means of earning a living. He could be seen here and there, wearing his only gallabiya, always smiling and content, until his skinny frame needed some rest; then he would head for the cellar and stretch out on his bed on the ground, not far from the gate to the old fort.

One day he saw a donkey pulling a cart. It was about to crush a tiny cat that was playing in the street. 'Stop!' he cried out without even thinking. However, that shout of his startled Sheikh Asfouri who was making his way towards the square. Fearful and suspicious, he stood still, muttering: 'I seek refuge in God'. He was a man who truly believed in hidden secrets. Just then, a huge stone crashed to the ground just a few feet in front of him. He had no idea how it had fallen or where from. It was obvious to everyone who witnessed the incident that, if Sheikh Asfouri had not stopped in reaction to the Son of the Quarter's shout, the stone would have crushed him. The sheikh uttered a prayer, almost fainting in shock. He then stared fixedly at the Son of the Quarter.

'I hereby swear that you are a good man,' he said humbly. 'Part of God resides within you.'

People believed what he said. The status of the Son of the Quarter now rose from that of virtual vagrant to sainthood or semi-sainthood. Loving eyes now watched over him as he went to and fro, and he received plenty of pennies and bits of bread. Some people did their best to discover his secret, but he never responded, nor did he claim to know something that he did not. Everyone grew to respect him; they said that his wondrous deeds were a sign of his tongue's revelation of God's own will. With every passing day he earned a yet surer place in the hearts of people until he came to know them and they him.

One night he went back to his bed on the ground in the cellar. But, before the angel of sleep could take over, a profound silence descended, one that augured some unforeseen event. The Son of the Quarter looked all around him, not understanding what was happening. Just then, a deep voice, clear and impressive, came from above:

'Son of the Quarter,' it intoned, 'go to Boss Zawi and tell him to give back every illegitimate penny he owes to the people who deserve it.'

At first, he had the idea that someone was playing a trick on him, but he dismissed the thought when he recalled the feelings that had come over him and the strange tones of the voice that penetrated to his very core. Now he was afraid. He was afraid even though he was used to being alone in the dark and sleeping close to the old fort, where the quarter's demon had resided since time immemorial.

'Who's speaking?' he asked as he sat there in the dark.

When the echo bounced back from the corner of the cellar, he was jolted awake and fully conscious. He kept hoping that the whole thing was a dream or illusion, but then the same voice came back with even more force:

'Son of the Quarter, go to Boss Zawi and tell him to give back every illegitimate penny he owes to the people who deserve it.'

He realised with a shiver that the voice he was

hearing was too strong, clear and strange to belong to anyone in the quarter. Perhaps it was his turn now to contact the inhabitants of the old fort, as many people in the quarter had been called to do. That meant that he had to obey the command, in spite of Boss Zawi's status in the community and the fact that he had been kind to him on more than one occasion. He had to obey the command. For a moment he hesitated, but then he felt the proximity of the voice's threatening tone. With new resolve he stood up immediately and walked on his way with limitless confidence. Eventually he stopped in front of Sheikh Zawi, who was sitting between the Sheikh of the Quarter and the mosque Imam by the café. The three men stopped smoking, and Zawi looked at the Son of the Quarter.

'What's with you?' he asked. 'Are you starving?'

'I bring you a command from the old fort,' he replied firmly. 'A voice has told me to come to you and tell you to give back every single illicit penny you owe to the people who deserve it.'

They were all so stunned that, for a short while, their tongues were tied. Boss Zawi was the first to recover. Walking round the narguileh pipe, he slapped the Son of the Quarter on the cheek. Then, shouting at the top of his voice, he sent him hurtling into the middle of the square. The Head of the Quarter took him back to his seat. Everyone watching the scene unfold looked furious, all of them well aware of Zawi's temper. The Son of the Quarter staggered away, telling himself that the voice must be toying with him; it probably belonged to a nasty demon. People spread the news, but they were all inclined to believe that the voice belonged to one of the honest, believing demons. Otherwise, how could his opinions about Zawi and his wealth mirror their own so closely?

It was only a few days later that the voice came back to harass the Son of the Quarter. When he heard it, he went into a panic and sat there in the dark.

'I'd be completely crazy,' he said miserably, 'if I were to obey you again.'

Once again, the voice echoed in the cellar's void, telling him to go to see Zawi, and so on.

'If it's so important to you,' he pleaded, 'then why don't you do it yourself? You're much stronger, and I'm just a poor wretch a thousand times over.'

Brooking no argument, the voice insistently repeated its blunt instruction.

The Son of the Quarter jumped to his feet, unable to bear his own impotence. He felt a new burst of courage and resolve, as though he had downed a whole bottle of wine. Everyone was astounded when they saw him coming, and Zawi glared at him as he pushed away the narguileh pipe. People spending the evening in the café were transfixed by the man with only one gallabiya.

'Go away, and there won't be any trouble,' the Head of the Quarter warned.

However, the Son of the Quarter still shouted his message at Zawi:

'The voice tells you to give back every single illicit penny you owe to the people who deserve it.'

Zawi pounced on him, pummelling his face and kicking his body until he fell to the ground, writhing and moaning as blood poured from his nose and mouth.

Then something happened that was a rare event in the quarter. The people who were sitting stood up, and others watching came over to prevent the Son of the Quarter from being hurt further. In the scramble, they grew more and more angry and found themselves engaged in a bloody battle.

As the mosque Imam described it, it was indeed a black night. The place was filled with furious people, blood flowed and Zawi fell just as the Son of the Quarter had before. The Head of the Quarter, amazed at the sheer number of people wounded, stood up to restore order.

'What an incredible night!' the Head of the Quarter said to the Imam. 'Even stranger than the story of the demons in the old fort.'

NABQA IN THE OLD FORT

Nabqa was the last son of Adam, the water-seller. He fathered him after nine others had died in the great plague. He pledged his son to the service of the local mosque, if God should allow him to live. He fulfilled that pledge by handing over his son to the mosque's Imam when he was seven years old.

'Service in God's own house is the best kind,' he told his friends. 'Between prayers, supplications, and studies, his heart will imbibe both light and blessing.'

Nabqa spent most of his time in the mosque, much less in his own home or with the boys in the quarter. The Imam was very pleased with him and praised both his energy and his reliability. He was now almost ten years old, but at that time he suffered the death of both his parents. He was known for being particularly fond of the old fort over the cellar.

'When is the fort inside the cellar open?' he would ask anyone who happened to pass by.

'It's usually open once a year,' would be the almost universal response, 'when the archaeologists come. But now it's turned into a haven for demons.'

When Nabqa was ten years old, the Imam allowed him to visit his parents' grave.

'It's not the season for visiting graves,' he told the boy.

But the boy insisted, using as an excuse a dream he had had. He went, but did not return as expected; he was away for three whole days. The Imam became alarmed and assumed that the boy had chosen a new path for his life; either that, or else something had happened to him. He told the Head of the Quarter about his worries, and the Sheikh sent a guard to look for the boy. But, just a few hours before the end of the third day, he saw the boy coming back from the cellar. He had a serene expression his face that did not match his egregious misbehaviour.

'Where have you been?' the Imam asked him angrily.

'I was a guest of the departed,' he responded calmly. 'They've filled me with knowledge and strength.'

'Have you gone mad, Nabqa?' the Imam asked him, looking baffled. 'Or has a demon affected you?'

'God's farewell to you! I'm leaving.'

'Where are you going?'

'It's not right for me to be your servant any more, nor for you to be my master.'

'God's curse on you!' the Imam shouted.

From that moment on the quarter learned the other side of Nabqa, the water-seller's son.

People were shocked by how brazen his behaviour had become, something none of them expected of a boy of his young age or even a madman. He began to confront important people from the quarter and usually addressed them with phrases like:

'You should be ashamed of yourself!'

'How could you let yourself do that?'

'Are you still feigning self-respect?'

After opening gambits such as these, he would go on to mention some moral or financial scandal. The result would be angry shouting. People wondered where the boy managed to get hold of these secrets. Their negative reactions took all possible forms: there were intrigues and enmities, and panic spread far and wide. There was good reason to say that the quarter had been struck by a demon. The entire affair was hard on the mosque's Imam; he considered himself somehow responsible for what was happening. The widespread negative reaction affected him too, and he decided to go to see Nabqa.

'Go back to your mosque!' he shouted.

'You go back to *your* mosque!' the boy yelled even louder. 'I don't have one anymore.'

The Imam accused the boy of heresy. He pounced on him, fully intending to use force. However, the boy was able to push him off, using a new power acquired from the unknown. Losing his balance, the Imam staggered backwards, quivering with fright. The Head of the Quarter came rushing over.

'Get to the quarter fast,' the Imam said, 'before it loses its reputation for ever.'

'I've never uttered a false word,' the boy insisted.

'The law must be respected,' the Head of the Quarter shouted back.

'You don't respect yourself,' the boy replied, working himself into a frenzy. 'So how can you ask people to respect the law?'

That made the Head of the Quarter furious, and he attacked the boy with his cane. He did it lightly at first, but the boy paid no attention and did not move. When he started hitting him harder, the boy just stood there calmly while everyone watched in dismay. It looked as if the boy was only getting stronger and more able to absorb the blows. Something other-worldly was happening right in front of them all.

Afterwards, the things I heard about Nabqa's story were fragmented and exaggerated accounts of his strange behaviour. There was one confused account about a fight that broke out in the quarter, involving all sorts of people. It lasted all day, only fizzling out in the evening when waves of darkness descended. People said that Nabqa was arrested, and that people trampled on him. However, grave-dwellers were able to confirm that he was still alive. They had seen him wandering around the area beyond the cellar. With every step he took, he grew bigger and bigger until he took up so much space that they could no longer see his head as it extended into the heavens.

And still today, people believe Nabqa is living in the old fort.

THE SCREAM

One day at noontime, there was a resounding scream, one with blood-curdling depths, as if a body were being ripped apart. The screaming continued, so people rushed towards Sitt Adliya's house. There was a lot of noise, everyone was shouting; a scene of chaotic activity. However, the noise did not last for long; it gradually died down, then stopped altogether. Everything went quiet, and silence prevailed. A voice went up announcing the end. The news spread like wildfire: Kamila, the lovely girl who had been divorced at noontime that very day, had poured petrol over her clothes and set fire to herself.

'God damn Satan the accursed,' said Umm Ulwan, neighbour of Sitt Adliya, the aunt of the girl who had immolated herself. 'Who would believe what we've just seen? Who could believe that Kamila would set fire to herself? What a lovely girl she was! Ever since she was ten years old, she always did everything that was asked of her. A bride just a few months on from her wedding night... Dear Kamila, was there ever a woman more deserving of life than you?'

Sitt Adliya, the girl's aunt, dried her tears.

'Your screams and the image of your face disfigured by fire are seared into my heart,' she said, 'May God avenge you on Zaid al-Fiqi, the despicable tyrant whose heart has turned to stone. What can this innocent girl have done to make him break her heart and divorce her? God will deal with you, Zaid!'

When these words reached Boss Zaid al-Fiqi, he said nothing. Truth to tell, the news of the girl's suicide had hit him and his heart very hard and addled his thinking. For a few moments, he grew weary of life and despised it. But then he pushed such sorrows away.

'What was I supposed to do,' he asked himself, 'once I found out what everyone already knew?' Everyone in the quarter knew that his wife's mother owned a brothel in the district. She had not in fact married a Moroccan, as her sister, Sitt Adliya, had announced, and gone away with him, leaving her daughter, Kamila, for her aunt to look after. 'Relatives asked questions about the story, and friends advised me to watch out for my reputation and avoid any damage to my business. Every time I spoke to someone about the family involved in the marriage, they would say that they knew absolutely nothing.'

'We're respectable people,' Sitt Adliya told him. 'We haven't deceived you.'

Kamila herself was thunderstruck. 'I don't believe it,' she cried. 'My mother's a decent woman. God protect us all from liars!'

'What could I do? When my own mother confirmed that they had all lied and deceived me in their desire to get hold of my money, I was convinced. For the sake of my own honour I was forced to get angry, so I roared like a wild animal and divorced my wife. And now she's committed suicide ... She was certainly telling the truth. She knew absolutely nothing about her mother's way of life. Hassan Abu al-Makarim, that virtuous sheikh, was the only one aware of that secret life. Everything goes back to God.'

It is true that Sheikh Abu al-Makarim, the Arabic language teacher, was the one who had sneaked the information into the quarter and worked to see that it reached Zaid al-Fiqi, the blind husband. It had not been an easy decision to make, and the sheikh only proceeded after a lengthy dialogue with his heart and conscience. It is my belief that, in making this decision, he was defending the truth and basing his judgment on principles far removed from his own heart and desires. When he heard about the girl's suicide, he was stunned, so stunned that it tore him from his roots. He panicked, as though being pursued.

'How can it be,' he asked himself, 'that the very worst crime committed by despair in this whole affair was setting fire to that lovely face?'

Sheikh Abu al-Makarim's distress triggered memories that now emerged from their hiding-places.

The first day he had ever set eyes on her, she was accompanying her aunt on a visit to Sitt Umm Hanafi, who owned the house in which he was living. Umm Hanafi had noticed how his demeanour changed and was well aware of his inherent simplicity and innocence.

'Did you like Kamila?' she asked him once.

'She's a precious angel!' he replied with a laugh.

'How lucky is the person,' she said, 'who can bring two people together in marriage.'

But he asked her to wait until he felt ready.

Afterwards she passed his name on to Sitt Adliya, Kamila's aunt. It seemed that things would take their normal course.

At this point he recalled that people had advised

him to do some checking to find out all the details. He postponed the actual engagement for a while. While they were all waiting, Sheikh Zaid al-Fiqi, boasting all the temptations of wealth and luxury, presented himself to Sitt Adliya. So, the hesitant sheikh was abandoned and Kamila was married to Zaid al-Fiqi.

Sheikh Abu al-Makarim was very sad; the world darkened before him. He felt utterly humiliated, his traditional sense of dignity was insulted.

'They sold me off,' he told Umm Hanafi, 'as though I was worth nothing.'

'You waited too long,' she replied, by way of consolation. 'Everything is fated.'

It was at this point that the chief sweeper of the quarter told him the shocking details about Kamila's mother. Along with shock came another sensation, but he rejected it out of hand. He pondered what to do.

'Let the verdict be based on the truth and decent morals,' he told himself. 'Whatever has happened has happened and let the consequences be what they may.'

Abu al-Makarim was shocked by the suicide and would have liked to run away. But where would he go? No sooner did he escape one personal hell than he fell into another. Eventually he found some relief in imitating the tortured screams that had emerged from the lovely girl's throat.

Umm Hanafi testified that the sheikh had gone mad long before everyone else realised it.

NAMLA'S PROPHESY

On the blessed night of the Prophet's birthday, Haraq
left the cellar, prodding the ground with his cane.

'Charity for God, you charitable folk!' he shouted
in a weak but determined tone.

On his way to the square, Namla, the local madman,
stopped him by the fountain.

'Good news, Haraq,' the madman yelled in a tone
of voice used by those trained to speak up first.

'On this joyous night,' the beggar replied, 'release
me from your tongue!'

'No, it's good news for a hero,' the madman insisted.
'People will surround you, and rulers will come to see
you!'

Some people heard this prophesy and had a good
laugh. Even the Head of the Quarter joined in.

'So now it's Haraq's turn,' he whispered, 'to ascend
the ruler's throne!'

Later that same night, Haraq fell down dead in

a corner that was teeming with people celebrating. Was he hit by accident, or crushed by the crowd? God alone knows.

People clustered around the dead body, but then the authorities showed up, one after another: the police officer, the chief prosecutor, and the official doctor.

The Head of the Quarter rubbed his hands together.

'You're a genuine saint, Namla,' he said. 'You gave your prophecy and it came true. The miracle happened.'

BAD LUCK

Three times Hassan Dahshan married girls from quarter families, and each time the wife died before giving birth to the baby inside her. Afterwards Hassan was known as 'Unlucky Hassan.' When he became engaged to a fourth girl, who died while they were still betrothed, the label stuck and became even more widely used. He was assailed by a peculiar feeling, one that told him to run away, to retreat from the world and become an ascetic. His family advised him not to give up and encouraged him to move beyond his bad luck.

'All's well,' they told him, 'that ends well!'

He responded to their suggestion and made one or two more attempts, but all doors were firmly closed against him. In spite of his family's status and his own wealth, people considered him the very Angel of Death. He withdrew and lived alone, hating life itself, friendless, and practising his trade without enthusiasm.

At that same time, Sunbula joined the household as a personal servant to his mother, whose energy and movement had been impaired by old age. Sunbula was approaching puberty, but she was also filthy and utterly destitute. Hassan's mother took pity on the girl after she lost her mother, the pickled vegetable seller, who herself had been the object of Hassan's mother's sympathy. As was her custom with female servants, she trained her to be tidy and would use her cane to set her straight, her aim being to make her acceptable. There was no way of turning a beanpole into a beautiful bride, and yet life flowed through the girl and showed its true colours. She learned how to comb her hair and started to learn more important things.

Even though she was neither beautiful nor alluring, Unlucky Hassan paid her close attention; he felt a strange warmth emerging from her. When he gestured to her, she responded without hesitation. He may have been eager in his first approach, but he felt repulsed as he left. Looking back over what he had suffered, the sheer misery of it all, he was appalled by this feeling, which only continued and intensified.

'No beauty,' he told himself, 'no money, and no morals.'

For long intervals their relationship continued

as it was, but, as time went by, he noticed that she was changing. She no longer wore such a vacant expression, and her eyes looked sad; it was as if she now understood why he would approach her but then retreat in disgust. He felt as though he were revealing himself in front of her, and that made him sad. When he gestured to her, she would not respond, but instead took refuge in the old woman's room.

'So,' he told himself, 'even vermin have their pride!' Her rejection infuriated him.

He realised that, over time, his mother had taught her a lot. He was amazed to learn that she had now begun to pray and to fast.

Once he grabbed her by the hand and pulled her forcibly towards him.

'I've enough misery to deal with,' she told him as she slipped from his grasp.

He had the feeling that what she had just said was true about both of them.

'So have I,' he told her. 'Each of us needs the other.'

SHAIKHUN

Shaikhun came back to the quarter after an absence so long he had been forgotten. Nothing was known about his absence, and all news about him had been severed. His family had all died, except for an old man who was not even conscious of his surroundings. Shaikhun was full of confidence, looking around him and offering inspiring words of blessing.

'When did he become a saint?' people asked in amazement. 'Someone favoured by God?'

He attracted people's attention, spreading joy to many hearts. The quarter's elite regarded him cautiously and with no particular interest, but they still refused to interfere.

Shaikhun now expanded his activities, venturing into the unknown, curing illnesses and solving the problems of the world's sufferers. On market day, he placed himself by the animal trough.

'Before the sun sets tomorrow,' he shouted at the

top of his voice, 'everyone will come to terms with their anxieties.'

By late afternoon, the quarter was crowded with people seeking cures. Their feelings were as one.

'This man's the son of an honest man.'

'Something unprecedented is sure to happen.'

Shaikhun arrived from the café, surrounded by a galaxy of admirers.

He looked around at the crowd, unperturbed by its size.

He raised his hand and silence fell.

'Hear a wonderful word,' he said, 'before a wonderful event.'

They all rejoiced and praised God before the silence of anticipation and longing descended.

A group of men now broke through the throng, led by the Head of the Quarter. When they reached the spot where Shaikhun was standing, two of them grabbed him. Between them, they put on him the gallabiyah for runaway lunatics.

'You really are a tiresome man!' said the Head of the Quarter.

THE ARROW

In spite of everything I have seen and heard, I know of
no parallel to the period in our quarter's life that has
become known as 'the black period.' It was a strange
time, one that our quarter had not experienced before,
nor has it since. The best description of it may well
be what Umm Fahim, the clothes presser, had to say,
namely that she had been touched by seven devils. I'll
never forget the day I asked a friend of mine with
more experience of life:

'What's going on beneath our very eyes?'

'It's obvious,' he replied regretfully, 'that the times
people are living through get sick and die just like all
the rest of God's creatures.'

What was odd was that it was not something awful
that no one knew about, but that no one felt ashamed
to openly discuss its evil effects. I heard Umm Basima,
the midwife, talk about it sarcastically:

'We'll be seeing fornicators naked in the sunshine,

and robbers committing theft with policemen watching.'

Every day we simply gave up, letting the tide sweep us away. Whenever we felt regretful, we would hastily invoke memories of our wonderful past. The Head of the Quarter kept up his efforts, or at least that was the impression he gave. He would leave his shop and crisscross the quarter from the cellar to the square.

'No offender will escape the law!' he would shout whenever the occasion permitted.

The police guard did not reduce his night watch, and the mosque Imam started chasing shadows with homilies, proverbs and tales of pious ancestors.

But then the death of Boss Zain al-Barak happened, fanning the flames of alarm and curiosity. It was market day, or 'a day for pillage and plunder' as everyone called it. The place was heaving with bargains, flirtations and curses. Boss Zain al-Baraka came strutting past on his grey donkey, with his servant walking ahead shouting: 'Make way, you! Here's Boss Zain al-Baraka!'

In front of the café the Boss let out a scream that augured ill. He tried to dismount but failed. Twisting around, he collapsed on to the saddle. People came rushing over and carried him to the café's nearest bench, drops of blood marking his course. The Head of the Quarter came hurrying to examine the Boss. He wept over him, making no sound, and then stood up straight.

'The divine secret has left him,' he said forlornly. 'Boss Baraka is dead.'

Even though everyone agreed that the Boss was nasty, the majesty of death provoked feelings of humility and awe in the people's hearts. The Head of the Quarter stared at them.

'No one went near him,' more than one voice opined.

'The police, chief prosecutor, and official doctor are going to go crazy,' he said angrily.

The most amazing thing the initial investigation showed was that the Boss had been shot through the heart with an arrow. Most people did not even know what was meant by the word 'arrow.' There was a good deal of chatter before people understood.

'Arrows are fired from a bow,' the Head of the Quarter explained. 'The person with the bow can't stand very far away. Many of you must have seen the culprit committing his crime.'

However, with solemn oaths they all claimed they had not seen anyone.

'I'm well aware,' said the Head of the Quarter

angrily, 'that Zain al-Baraka was not liked by many people...'

'They're far too many to count,' a voice stated, 'but we can only testify to what we know.'

The sheikh went all around the place, checking on houses that overlooked the site, but he did not come across anything suspicious.

'Who on earth would take an arrow out of history's quiver,' he kept asking himself, 'and why?'

The search went on for several days, but without success. All that was clear was the apathy and ill will people bore each other and their lack of confidence in the authorities and the law. When those in touch with the visible world were unable to quench the thirst for truth that people were feeling, those connected to the unseen volunteered to reveal the unknown.

'Don't forget the old fort,' said Sheikh Ramadan, saint of God. People do not forget their old fort, which was situated above the cellar.

'In the old days,' Sheikh Ramadan went on, 'the place was teeming with people carrying bows and arrows. It's not impossible for some power to have sent one of their spirits to defend our wretched quarter.' The idea spread and was on everyone's tongue. Just then, Umm Basima, the midwife, confirmed that when she was returning home after delivering a baby beyond the cellar, she had seen a shadow slinking along the wall by the fort.

The Head of the Quarter had the idea that some criminals might be using the fort as a hiding-place. He recruited some archaeologists and police to go with him. They entered the fort through the gate and searched the whole place. All they found were rocks and spiders.

They announced their findings loud and clear, and then warned people not to believe superstitions.

People looked at each other.

'Are we supposed to believe this lot,' they asked in disbelief, 'and disbelieve Sheikh Ramadan, saint of God, and the good lady, Sitt Basima?'

THE WHISPER OF THE STARS

The spray from the hose-wagon splashed his skinny bare feet as he ran behind it, shrieking and whooping. His grandmother managed to grab him by the public fountain and clasp him in her arms.

'You keep chasing things that will hurt you,' she said.

While she was pronouncing 'In the name of God' over his head, he kept protesting loudly. The Head of the Quarter noticed her and came over.

'Sitt Farga,' he told her, 'keep him away from things that will really hurt him.'

'Evil tongues never show us any mercy,' she replied angrily.

'But in your house he'd have the best possible education.'

'People's tongues will never show any mercy. One day, he's bound to find out about the tragedy of his mother and father.'

'Our quarter will never change its ways,' he replied sadly. 'So why don't you take him somewhere else, where there's no past to deal with?'

The woman closed her bleary eyes. 'Where and how could we live so far away from our quarter?'

'Well then, Sitt Farga,' the Head of the Quarter said, 'it's just a matter of fate!'

'Yes indeed, by our Lord, merciful and compassionate!'

Sheikh Bashir emerged from the mosque to get some fresh air. Farga spotted him and walked over, bringing her furious grandson with her.

'Shaikh Bashir,' she said, 'take my grandson's skull-cap and tell me about his future.'

'I can never forget his father's many virtues,' the sheikh replied, 'nor my fond memories of him. I'm always ready to help you, Sitt Farga.'

He sniffed the skull-cap and wiped his hands on the boy's head.

'I see only clouds,' he said.

'What does that mean?' she asked in alarm.

'I see only clouds. There's no more to say.'

'Yes there is, but you don't want to upset me.'

'Certainly not! Even so, you're aware of the dangers. You should be careful.'

Grandmother and grandson now walked away, although she was not happy.

The Head of the Quarter turned to Sheikh Bashir.

'What harm would it have done,' he asked, 'to tell her something comforting?'

'Maybe we can be selective in what we pass on,' he replied, 'but we can't tell lies. That's exactly what I told Qadri, the boy's late father, but he ignored my advice. Then what happened happened.'

The Head of the Quarter stared at him anxiously.

'How was that?' he asked.

'Do you remember one afternoon,' Sheikh Bashir told him, 'when the local Rebec poet showed up, so young and handsome, and started singing:

'Lovers have all left their beds ...'

'The whole quarter gave him a rousing welcome, and soon the owner of the local café invited him to perform at his soirées, where he generated an all-encompassing rapture that seized everyone's hearts. The man kept singing, and the quarter was both dazzled and delighted. But then I sensed a disturbance in my private world. I waited until I saw Boss Qadri approaching. I blocked his path.

'The falcon will pounce on the chicken,' I told him.

'He paid no attention to what I said. He assumed I

was asking him for money. With his usual generosity he gave me something.'

'Didn't he ask you what you meant?' the Head of the Quarter asked.

'No, it didn't seem to bother him.'

'Why didn't you reveal what fate was keeping hidden?'

'We can never cross that line. Or else we lose the blessing!'

'Then what happened?'

'The singer of love songs vanished, and Sitt Badriyya, the rich old merchant's wife went with him. The man was left with a one-year-old baby. The episode astounded the entire quarter, and our august merchant dropped dead.'

For a few moments there was silence.

'Perhaps the man and woman will both be dead,' the Head of the Quarter said, 'before the young boy can get his revenge.'

'God is all-knowing.'

'So what is the meaning of the clouds you mentioned to the grandmother?'

'It means that our knowledge involves uncertainty and temptation. But we should leave it to all-knowing God.'

OUR FATHER IGWA

All throughout his life his friends and peers had died; he was left with no friends or colleagues. This was Igwa, the lance-maker. His sons had died too, except for Anwar who was over eighty. The two of them shared the old house not far from the cellar. For a long time, they had not exchanged a single word; they simply stared at each other in silence, like strangers. However, the son had a problem with his legs. Needing to take a walk every few days, he had to have someone to lean on. So his father would come, give him his arm, and take him for a walk from the cellar to the fountain. All the while, people looked on in amazement.

Even so, time managed to devour his flesh, his fat, his teeth, and three-quarters of his sight and hearing. He could still eat, chew, and bring a smile to people's faces; and sometimes wrath and anger too.

'Someone who, by living so long, eats his way through all youth's deadlines!'

The day of the auction to sell off the endowments' ruined property was a day to remember.

It began with an attack of sickness that kept his son, Anwar, confined to bed.

People attending the auction were surprised when Igwa, the lance-maker, showed up carrying a small suitcase.

The Head of the Quarter, who was bidding for the land, stared at him in astonishment. He could not help himself.

'Wouldn't it be better,' he asked Igwa, 'if you stayed with your sick son?'

'I've left him in the care of someone whose attention makes any other need redundant,' was Igwa's firm reply.

'Why don't you leave the land to someone else?' the Head of the Quarter asked angrily. 'Then he will profit from it as well as other people.'

'Tomorrow I'm coming to an agreement with a building contractor,' Igwa said. 'Before a year's over, I will profit from it and so will other people.'

THE STORM

It all happened when the sun was high in the sky. The day was temperate and calm.

'My heart keeps warning me,' said Sheikh Bahiyya, for no particular reason, 'something sinister's about to happen.'

At that moment we heard a soft whining, which kept up without pausing for breath. Gathering energy, it rose and fell, but then became stronger and stronger, an increasingly violent dust storm that whistled through every nook and cranny, its echoes sounding like animals howling.

More than one voice shouted: 'O God, your forgiveness and mercy!'

However, now it was a roaring hurricane, bringing with it dust and different colours, to which everything rapidly succumbed. Containers, cages, and chickens flew off roofs, doors and windows slammed, screams and tears mingled. Meows, barks and brays all blended into one. With every passing minute, the chaos intensified and spread.

Voices escaped their usual confines:

'This must be Judgment Day.'

'We won't find any houses left standing.'

'This is how Satan reveals his secrets.'

The elemental violence continued until everyone was petrified and convinced that the end was undoubtedly near. Panic gripped the Head of the Quarter's mind and heart. In order to satisfy himself that he was doing his job properly, he started shouting instructions that were lost in the raging noise:

'Close your shops! Close doors and windows! No one should stay in the street!'

He made his way to the mosque courtyard and exchanged a despairing look with the Imam.

'What are you going to do, Head of the Quarter?' one of the refugees in the mosque asked him.

'We'll start work once the storm dies down,' he replied angrily.

'But we've never seen anything like this before.'

'I'm not responsible for winds,' he said.

They began to imagine a number of possibilities. Copious tears flowed. One man was eager to share in the unknown, and started telling the people with him about a dream he had had the day before, as the storm grew more and more violent. Another man who had reached the limits of despair shouted that we should forget about dreams. Reality had now surpassed any dream.

The storm raged until sunset; some people said, until nightfall. It went away just as it had arrived – no guesswork, no conjectures. Good God! The world resorted to heavy silence, as though that same silence were an expression of regret. Now there arose the din of survival as lights started to shine from windows and corners. The entire quarter heaved one huge, long sigh, one in which every single soul participated.

'What's lost is lost,' said Sheikh Bahiyya with a sob. 'It can be replaced.'

The Head of the Quarter grew angry.

'That's enough doom and gloom!' he yelled. 'Everyone has had enough.'

But the voices that reacted were tinged with despair. Destruction, looting, robbery, money gone, reputations lost.

The Head of the Quarter became more and more worried as he listened to these comments. Some of them confirmed that robbers had indeed crawled out of ditches, holes and utterly unexpected places. There were so many and they were so concentrated that they blocked out the sun. They had taken full advantage of the storm blowing; indeed some people claimed that they were the ones who had stirred it up and called it down from its usual place in the skies.

All this caused a ruckus and great sorrow. The feeling of desperation no longer discriminated between Sheikh Bahiya and the Head of the Quarter.

A small group of people, whose clothes were still white, gathered by the door of the old fort. They were exchanging whispers, shaking hands in the dark, waiting resolutely and impatiently for dawn.

THE END OF BOSS SAQR

That night, reality hit like a dream. Boss Saqr, aged seventy, with his bride Halima, aged twenty, arrived at the second floor of his house to usher in the first of his honeymoon nights. On the floor below, his first wife, the mother of his children, was sitting with her son, Ragab. They were silent and morose, sharing thoughts. The mother felt crushed by mountains of anxiety, while Ragab's face was flushed with anger.

'Unbelievable!' he said, staring at the ceiling.

'These days,' his aged mother replied, 'everything's unbelievable.'

'It's likely to collapse very soon.'

'I pray to God that he's still got a bit of sense.'

'What's scary is that all his money is in the safe in his bedroom.'

'He'll never forget that he's responsible for five girls and a boy.'

'I'm really sorry,' Ragab shouted angrily, 'that I

never learned anything, or went to work.'

'You're his only son,' she replied. 'He didn't want to overburden you.'

'If he were really concerned about me,' he said, 'he would not be committing my fate to the mercy of a rapacious girl.'

'Don't get angry. We'll only lose.'

'We must do something.'

'Think carefully. There has to be some kind of hope.'

The young man thought for a while.

'The solution is for him to give me, my sisters and you our legal due.'

'That's a reasonable request, but it will make him angry.'

'If we get scared, we'll lose out.'

'We have to act sensibly, otherwise it'll be two defeats, not one.'

All their lives, father and son had enjoyed everything that was fine and wonderful. Until this young girl had come along, his father had loved him more than anything else in the whole world. With that intense love, he had spoiled him, corrupted him, left him to face the world with no knowledge and no job. The safe had served as his security, until this girl had it clutched to her bosom. From now on, there was no hope.

Ragab found a potential outlet with the Head of
the Quarter. He respected him as an old friend of his
father's, so he went to see him and shared his worries.

'Forgive me for asking you,' he told the Head of the
Quarter, 'but it's better that you talk to him.'

'Out of respect for neighbourliness and affection,'
he replied, 'I'll do my very best. May God grant me
success!'

After Friday prayers, the Head of the Quarter took
the Boss aside and offered him advice about what
would be just and correct. The Boss was furious.

'Do they want to inherit from me before I'm dead?'
he shouted. 'This is the Devil's handiwork!'

Ragab expected his father to summon and upbraid
him. But instead, he ignored his son and cut him off.
This affected him deeply; he was haunted by fears,
awake and asleep. He made up his mind to defend
himself, his mother and his sisters. He was pondering
what he needed to do, but events anticipated him.
Boss Saqr returned home from an anniversary party
to find the house and the safe empty. Such was his
fury that people soon heard the news: it became clear
that the girl had run off with her cousin. Friends and
neighbours in the quarter spread out to search for
them, but Boss Saqr collapsed between life and death

and took the wretched crew back to his room.

'He's going to abandon us to ruin,' Ragab whispered in his mother's ear.

'We need to take care of him now,' she replied sadly, 'and let God's will be done!'

The Boss now remained in a state of semi-consciousness, no longer regretting anything. In a moment of wakefulness he recognised his wife and children. His wife had the impression that he wanted to say something and put her ear close to his mouth.

'Over the bath,' he whispered.

The Boss died, but it was several days before calm returned to his house. All that time the family kept wondering what the dead man had meant by referring to the loft over the bath.

Ragab decided he needed to investigate his father's statement. He climbed the wooden ladder into the loft, holding a gas lamp. He was greeted by spiders' webs, but the mice scuttled off. His eager eyes spotted a chest resting in timeless tranquillity.

When opened, it revealed a pile of golden guineas.

LIFE IS A GAME

I was visiting Ali Zaidan to congratulate him on his latest promotion in the company.

'I've repented,' he said. 'May God forgive what's happened in the past.'

'I've heard you say that many times before,' I replied dubiously.

'But this time,' he told me confidently, 'it comes with a solid determination.'

'Did one of the players fold, I wonder, or have some of your companions been conspiring against you?'

'What's so powerful this time is that the feeling's taken control of me for no specific reason. I'm motivated to transform my rotten life and welcome a new one.'

When he awoke from his feverish vertigo, he discovered that he was almost in his fifties and a stranger in our world, with no money saved to depend on, but instead a career that reeked of ill repute. He started to keep me company and initiate conversation, so as to discover the world anew and involve himself in people's business and concerns.

'The most precious thing I lost at the gambling table,' he once told me, when he was at his most anxious, 'was my life, not the money.'

'Life begins at sixty,' I told him, by way of consolation.

'I want to get married,' he told me, in all seriousness.

'There's a suitable bride for every age,' I said.

'I've spoken to my sister, Afkar, because she was always the first one to urge me to get married. But I want to get married in the genuine sense.'

'What do you mean?'

'I'm not looking for left-overs from a parfumier! What I'd like is a young virgin bride, reasonably good-looking and with some education.'

'These days marriage is expensive,' I told him frankly.

'Things can be arranged,' he replied, his voice scornful, 'through an advanced contract backed by my salary, which is not at all bad.'

'That's fine then. Isn't there a woman in your life?'

'I've never had any time for love,' he replied with a laugh tainted by bitterness.

A joint effort now began involving Afkar Hanem and me. We would begin the conversation by talking about his position and salary; that certainly aroused the listener's appetite for more. But when his career was mentioned, eyebrows went up, accompanied by a scowl. No sooner was the name Ali Zaidan uttered than the cry 'You mean, that gambler?' assaulted our ears. In fact, I came to realise that some people, although willing to overlook theft and bribery, were appalled by gambling and gamblers.

This news had to be shared with my friend. He was both sad and sorry and I had the impression that he was ageing twice as fast as before.

'I'm not going to leave this world,' he challenged me, 'unless I'm a husband and father.'

'We needn't despair,' I replied amiably.

'Now I have something to depend on. I've been to visit Sheikh Labib, and he's read the unseen for me.'

I could not help laughing.

'I didn't realise you were someone who believed in such men,' I said.

'Despair can lead to worse than that,' he replied with a sigh.

Sheikh Labib was telling the truth. Sitt Dalal, of evil reputation, renowned in our quarter, had heard about my friend's problem. She had a twenty-year-old daughter, a model of both beauty and liberation, who was arousing the quarter's anger. Sitt Dalal now decided to add this discarded entity to her own family. She tossed Suad, the beautiful young girl, into the old man's path, unperturbed by the whispers, leers, and winks. The old man, who was angry and desperate, fell into the golden trap. He paid no attention to his family's protests and lost all his friends, instead becoming one of the quarter's most intriguing stories.

'I'm not going to let anyone ruin my happiness,' he told me with a meaningless laugh, 'now that this sudden opportunity has arisen.' Seizing my hands, he added, 'I'm grateful to you for sticking by me and giving me your friendship. I hope that you too are convinced: whenever you accept a glass, you drink it to the dregs.'

The years went by, and Ali Zaidan had a son and two daughters. When he retired, his children managed to distract him from his worsening poverty. With her beauty his wife distracted him from everything else. His house became proverbial. Whenever things were tough, he would say 'I'm still losing at the gambling table'.

LATE NIGHT SECRET

He returned to the quarter a little before dawn. The quarter seemed sound asleep, eyelids firmly shut. At that hour, his tottering shadow was all that was visible in the night's darkness. He progressed cautiously until he entered a field which gave off a magical scent. Where could this fragrant perfume be coming from? It was his senses that were roused to respond:

'The trail of a woman passing, the trace left by a female as she crossed from one side to the other. Why am I immersed in darkness at this time of night? On my own, guided only by my throbbing heart and an unknown destiny.'

His heart was filled with an aroma so sensually thrilling it overwhelmed him. For a while, his feet remained rooted to the ground, but then he began to walk slowly to and fro in the quarter as though he were a night watchman. Had he arrived a few minutes earlier, he might well have seen a rare sight in the final hours of the night. It might well have been something quite normal, far removed from his lively imagination.

Even so, he was still inclined to follow the wild idea that would conjure an adventure from this atmosphere. He expected some secret to be exposed in this quarter, so shrouded in piety and the counsels of the righteous. Morning or evening, whenever a woman passed by, he would remember, sniff, and sigh. Then he would sniff again.

THE PRAYER OF SHEIKH QAF

Umaira al-Ayiq had been murdered.

Hifni al-Rayiq was accused of the crime.

Al-Zayni, Kibrita, and Fayiq all witnessed the crime and testified to it.

Hifni al-Rayiq confessed to the crime. People looked amazed as they compared the victim's huge size with the tiny body of the killer.

'He pounced on me,' Hifni said, 'but I got away. I threw a stone at him, and it killed him.'

Those who do not believe in fate were prepared to believe him. In spite of the victim's status, people regarded the incident as closed. All that remained was to await the verdict.

But the quarter has its own hidden tongue, although no one knows to whom it belongs. It can whisper misgivings and reveal secrets. Such rumours persisted until they filled the entire atmosphere like a powerful smell. One such rumour, terse and obscure, stated that

Al-Rayiq did not murder Al-Ayiq; Al-Zaini, Kibrita, and Fayiq were all false witnesses. Not only that, but Al-Rayiq was falsely testifying against himself, as sometimes happens in our quarter's folklore.

'Have you heard what's being said about the Al-Ayiq murder?' the mosque Imam asked the Head of the Quarter.

'There's no end to our quarter's folktales,' the Head of the Quarter replied with a frown.

The Head of the Quarter slunk over to Sheikh Qaf's house, cradle of blessings and readings of the unseen.

'There's not a single man or woman in our quarter,' he said, approaching the Sheikh, 'who hasn't come to this room for a private consultation. You know a lot of things that we don't.'

'Praise be to the One who is all-knowing!' the Sheikh replied in his effeminate voice, acquired through his brotherly relationship with a female demon.

'Who killed Umaira al-Ayiq?' the Head of the Quarter asked, using a hard stare to penetrate to his very depths.

'O ye who believe, do not ask about things that, if they were clear to you, would annoy you. God knows, and you do not.'

'But who murdered Umaira al-Ayiq?' the Head of the Quarter asked emphatically.

'Whoever's on your mind,' was the Sheikh's sad reply.

The Head of the Quarter clasped his cane even harder but said nothing. He stood up to leave.

'I'll spare you,' said Sheikh Qaf, 'by not asking what you plan to do.'

The Head of the Quarter still said nothing. He shook the Sheikh's hand in silence and moved towards the door.

'I raise a lengthy prayer to God,' the Sheikh said with uncharacteristic fervour, 'that I'll see you again.'

TAWHIDA

The White House is situated two houses before the cellar, to the right as you approach from the main square. The name was adopted because of the skin colour of the people who lived there.

Tawhida, you were the crown jewel in the white house. All praise to the One who created and formed you in the loveliest guise! Your beauty was peerless, although the vestiges of it that live in my imagination are far more vivid than the ones in my actual memory. For the most part, we only knew the members of the white house family from afar, but Tawhida was a God-bestowed exception because she joined our family through marriage. We came to know her intimately and to experience many of her virtues. Even though I was still very young, I was intoxicated by her rosy complexion, her black hair, and the sweet tone of her voice, which we all tried happily to imitate. At first we treated her with cautious respect, but soon the gates were opened. A growing familiarity dispensed with the blush of bashful cheeks. In fact, she had a genuine simplicity, she was pleasant, kind and happy. None of us has ever forgotten that a car would arrive at a fixed time every morning to take her to the European school. At the time, everyone in the quarter said that she had been Europeanised, something that was new, exciting, and provocative – indeed something to boast about. Now, however, she was living with us, speaking both French and Italian and wearing the latest fashions. She could repeat the ideas of Descartes and recite Baudelaire's poetry, play a piano piece by Beethoven from memory. But none of that made us envious, because she was so breathtakingly beautiful, always happy and always ready to tell us funny jokes. In addition to all that, she had shown us her other charming aspects: the lovely girl was also very fond of the voices of Munira, Abd al-Hayy, and Sayyid Darwish. She could play the Moonlight Sonata, but could also sing 'She has risen, and how lovely is her light!' She could memorise selections from the poetry of Shawqi and Hafiz, but even more impressively, she was very conscientious about praying and fasting during Ramadan and made a point of listening to famous reciters like Ali Mahmud and Nada. What was even more astonishing was that she gave Umm Ruqayya her hand.

'Tell me what the days keep concealed from us,' she asked.

No Beethoven, Descartes or Baudelaire could rob her heart of the legacy of her earlier years spent in the quarter. She still believed in incense and fortune-tellers, and, no doubt, in the existence of demons in the old fort above the cellar in our quarter.

The passage of time separated the different branches of our family tree, and we all went to the place that suited us. She went to Zamalek, then spent a period abroad, but came back. She became a mother, then a grandmother, but I did not see her for a long time. I did, however, retain fond memories of her as a young girl, when happiness, beauty and magic all came together in her.

I was sitting on the sidewalk by the Hotel Arnaud, staring over the corniche at the Mediterranean in the distance. A car stopped directly in front of me, and I spotted an old woman sitting beside the driver and waving at me. I did not recognise her. She had a face that might be an icon to old age: gaunt, pale, thin, and wrinkled. She was wearing dark glasses.

'Don't you recognise me?' she asked when she saw

how shocked and surprised I looked.

When I heard that sweet voice again, the past came rushing back like a perfume bottle smashing to the ground.

I stumbled my way over as fast as I could, feeling both abashed and nostalgic. We exchanged a few pleasantries, and I plunged into the remotest of memories.

'If you didn't recognise me,' she said with a laugh, 'it's not my fault!'

NAGUIB MAHFOUZ NOBEL PRIZE FOR LITERATURE ACCEPTANCE SPEECH

Stockholm 1988

Ladies and Gentlemen,

To begin with I would like to thank the Swedish Academy and its Nobel committee for taking notice of my long and perseverant endeavours, and I would like you to accept my talk with tolerance. For it comes in a language unknown to many of you. But it is the real winner of the prize. It is, therefore, meant that its melodies should float for the first time into your oasis of culture and civilisation. I have great hopes that this will not be the last time either, and that literary writers of my nation will have the pleasure to sit with full merit amongst your international writers who have spread the fragrance of joy and wisdom in this grief-ridden world of ours.

I was told by a foreign correspondent in Cairo that

the moment my name was mentioned in connection with the prize silence fell and many wondered who I was. Permit me, then, to present myself in as objective a manner as is humanly possible. I am the son of two civilisations that at a certain age in history have formed a happy marriage. The first of these, seven thousand years old, is the Pharaonic civilisation; the second, one thousand four hundred years old, is the Islamic one. I am perhaps in no need to introduce to any of you either of the two, you being the elite, the learned ones. But there is no harm, in our present situation of acquaintance and communion, in a mere reminder.

As for Pharaonic civilisation I will not talk of the conquests and the building of empires. This has become a worn out pride the mention of which modern conscience, thank God, feels uneasy about. Nor will I talk about how it was guided for the first time to the existence of God and its ushering in the dawn of human conscience. This is a long history and there is not one of you who is not acquainted with the prophet-king Akhenaton. I will not even speak of this civilisation's achievements in art and literature and its renowned miracles: the Pyramids and the Sphinx and Karnak. For he who has not had the chance to see these monuments has read about them and pondered over their forms.

Let me, then, introduce Pharaonic civilisation with what seems like a story since my personal circumstances have ordained that I become a storyteller. Hear, then, this recorded historical incident: old papyri relate that Pharaoh had learned of the existence of a sinful relation between some women of the harem and men of his court. It was expected that he should finish them off in accordance with the spirit of his time. But he, instead, called to his presence the choice men of law and asked them to investigate what he had come to learn. He told them that he wanted the truth so that he could pass his sentence with justice.

This conduct, in my opinion, is greater than founding an empire or building the pyramids. It is more telling of the superiority of that civilisation than any riches or splendour. Gone now is that civilisation – a mere story of the past. One day the great Pyramid will disappear too. But truth and justice will remain for as long as mankind has a ruminative mind and a living conscience.

As for Islamic civilisation, I will not talk about its call for the establishment of a union between all mankind under the guardianship of the creator, based on freedom, equality and forgiveness. Nor will I talk about the greatness of its prophet. For among your thinkers there are those who regard him the greatest man in history. I will not talk of its conquests, which have planted thousands of minarets calling for worship, devoutness and good throughout great expanses of land from the environs of India and China to the boundaries of France. Nor will I talk of the fraternity between religions and races that has been achieved in its embrace in a spirit of tolerance unknown to mankind neither before nor since.

I will, instead, introduce that civilisation in a moving dramatic situation summarising one of its most conspicuous traits: in one victorious battle against Byzantium, it gave back its prisoners of war in return for a number of books of the ancient Greek heritage in philosophy, medicine and mathematics. This is a testimony of value for the human spirit in its demand for knowledge, even though the demander was a believer in God and the demanded a fruit of a pagan civilisation.

It was my fate, ladies and gentlemen, to be born in the lap of these two civilisations, and to absorb their milk, to feed on their literature and art. Then I drank the nectar of your rich and fascinating culture. From the inspiration of all this – as well as my own anxieties – words bedewed from me. These words had the fortune to merit the appreciation of your revered Academy which has crowned my endeavour with the great Nobel Prize. Thanks be to it in my name and in the name of those great departed builders who have founded the two civilisations.

Ladies and Gentlemen,

You may be wondering: This man coming from the third world, how did he find the peace of mind to write stories? You are perfectly right. I come from a world labouring under the burden of debts whose paying back exposes it to starvation or very close to it. Some of its people perish in Asia from floods, others do so in Africa from famine. In South Africa, millions have been undone with rejection and with deprivation of all human rights in the age of human rights, as though they were not counted among humans. In the West Bank and Gaza there are people who are lost in spite of the fact that they are living on their own land; land of their fathers, grandfathers and great grandfathers. They have risen to demand the first right secured by primitive man; namely, that they should have their proper place recognised by others as their own. They were paid back for their brave and noble move – men, women, youths and children alike – by the breaking of bones, killing with bullets, destroying of houses and torture in prisons and camps. Surrounding them are 150 million Arabs following what is happening in anger and grief. This threatens the area with a disaster if it is not saved by the wisdom of those desirous of a just and comprehensive peace.

Yes, how did the man coming from the Third World find the peace of mind to write stories? Fortunately, art is generous and sympathetic. In the same way that it dwells with the happy ones it does not desert the wretched. It offers both alike the convenient means for expressing what swells up in their bosom.

In this decisive moment in the history of civilisation it is inconceivable and unacceptable that the moans of mankind should die out in the void. There is no doubt that mankind has at last come of age, and our era carries the expectations of *entente* between the superpowers. The human mind now assumes the task of eliminating all causes of destruction and annihilation. And just as scientists exert themselves to cleanse the environment of industrial pollution, intellectuals ought to exert themselves to cleanse humanity of moral pollution. It is both our right and duty to demand of the big leaders in the countries of civilisation as well as their economists to affect a real leap that would place them into the focus of the age.

In the olden times every leader worked for the good of his own nation alone. The others were considered adversaries or subjects of exploitation. There was no regard to any value but that of superiority and personal glory. For the sake of this, many morals, ideals and values were wasted; many unethical means were justified; many uncounted souls were made to perish. Lies, deceit, treachery, cruelty reigned as the signs of sagacity and the proof of greatness. Today, this view needs to be changed from its very source. Today, the greatness of a civilised leader ought to be measured by the universality of his vision and his sense of responsibility towards all humankind. The developed world and the Third World are but one family. Each human being bears responsibility towards it by the degree of what he has obtained of knowledge, wisdom, and civilisation. I would not be exceeding the limits of my duty if I told them in the name of the Third World: Be not spectators to our miseries. You have to play therein a noble role befitting your status. From your position of superiority you are responsible for any misdirection of animal, or plant, to say nothing of man, in any of the four corners of the world. We have had enough of words. Now is the time for action. It is time to end the age of brigands and usurers. We are in the age of leaders responsible for the whole globe. Save the enslaved in the African south! Save the famished in Africa! Save the Palestinians from the bullets and the torture! Nay, save the Israelis from profaning their great spiritual heritage! Save the ones in debt from the rigid laws of economy! Draw their attention to the fact that their responsibility to mankind should precede their commitment to the laws of a science that time has perhaps overtaken.

I beg your pardon, ladies and gentlemen, I feel I may have somewhat troubled your calm. But what do you expect from one coming from the Third World? Is not every vessel coloured by what it contains? Besides, where can the moans of mankind find a place to resound if not in your oasis of civilisation planted by its great founder for the service of science, literature and sublime human values? And as he did one day by consecrating his riches to the service of good, in the hope of obtaining forgiveness, we, children of the Third World, demand of the able ones, the civilised ones, to follow his example, to imbibe his conduct, to meditate upon his vision.

Ladies and Gentlemen,

In spite of all what goes on around us I am

committed to optimism until the end. I do not say with Kant that good will be victorious in the other world. Good is achieving victory every day. It may even be that evil is weaker than we imagine. In front of us is an indelible proof: were it not for the fact that victory is always on the side of good, hordes of wandering humans would not have been able in the face of beasts and insects, natural disasters, fear and egotism, to grow and multiply. They would not have been able to form nations, to excel in creativeness and invention, to conquer outer space, and to declare human rights. The truth of the matter is that evil is a loud and boisterous debaucherer, and that man remembers what hurts more than what pleases. Our great poet Abul-'Alaa' Al-Ma'ari was right when he said:

A grief at the hour of death
Is more than a hundred-fold
Joy at the hour of birth.

I finally reiterate my thanks and ask your forgiveness.

Read at the Swedish Academy by Mohamed Salmawy

SELECTED HANDWRITTEN STORIES

A selection of the stories in Naguib Mahfouz's original handwriting.

Your Lot in Life

The Arrow

The Whisper of the Stars

The Storm

نصيبك في الحياة

الدفعة لا تدري متى بدأت الظاهرة . كل شاهد يقص اسطورته فقد شاع ترتيبه
نقول لم نحفظ الغلا ، أصبحت للبيع الظاهرة لتشترى بثمرة بالسعر ، و أخذ الرجل
فكرة الجديد و جعل يبسط و الشارع بري تقصد للضعف باختار ، وإذا لم يكن عم حمل
نخلة و يجمع و البلاد ، و دخلت أنا عربت ، دخلت معايا ، و ما يطلب
بعده و كانه استمري كان ، و يبكي بيه ، و يتخطط و يواصل البكاء ، و يجمع
الناس ما هذا ركبه هذا هذا ، و أطلع جميده اليتيم و هذا لا بأس مع البكاء
و تقول أم بحاضرها باين من الحمل ، حياتي تمد ستم ادم على برهان لتكاره ، الخلل
و فيها صوتشين إلى البلاد ، والطفل ترتفت نخلة ، و صبيته بلاحظ ، و عملت
يبلغ جهارة ، و زينهم كانوا ما عمة ، و نظرة كل نفس الوقت فمكانى الوزن من
شتم ذا من هنا ، انطلقتي ، و حفقتا استوجبت صمدتي بأخطا ، و تجمع الناس
يرجع اليها زوجج من دكانة و رقص في إلى بشر ، والناس سيبنا دلوع النظرات الملتهبة
والاندماج و الدهشة ..

و تعددت الخطات و تنوعت ، و تولوا الضحايا من الرجال والنساء . و بلغ الجبن
شيخ الحارة فجاء به يناصبها

- لا يخفون من اقتسام الربح والمخدرات ..
وكانه سعادة . كانت عند اللوم و التفرج عندما شاهد فقيرا و هو
يجسم في البكاء ، انفال لدماء الزاوية .
- هذه نصيب جديدة في هذا رتما إلى لا تتبع من خلف المعاطيب ..
تعال الأمام
- الناس تدري دلالة لحيات الدائرة ، والمشروب بالطابة باردة
و إذا تم دهنية البطانة قريبة من الدين ، تدخلت فيه قائله
- لا علاج للحاله إلا بالأمر ..
شمالك الأمام
- و بايس دخل العناصر في البكاء ؟
نقال لك نصيب
- ليبكيان أناسا بلا سبب الد يبس من عفوية ، و لم يترك العفريت الد
بدته إلا ..
تعال شيخ الحارة جدا
- لا يوافقهم مع احتساب الحارة ملك مجمومة ، و كانى سانع الأمر
إلى شفى الصحة
و نهض الرجل إلى سعادة المفتى ذو لغة الأمر ، و قال المفتى

ـ وأنهم لا تعرفون بين المنفى والرهن ..

تجفله له بنفذة الدموع بعينيه ، وإنه لدغا ، فلو بيت سد دموع . من صباح
اليوم التالي زار المقبس الحارة مصحوبا بحراسة وتمويجية . ودخع اليه الناس
رغم بجوم ـ أنطلب لحضرة المنفش" . فومضى بمتباعده ، وتأمد متباصفه
سريعا ، أنطلب الدهشه عندما شاهد التلاميذ والكبار ، وسأله المفش شيخ الحرف
ـ أم يجد جديد في حياتنا كما سد أيور ؟ يسبب رؤيه ؟

ـ وبلا .. لا جديد .. حياتنا هي حياتنا حيراتنا واهذا لي ..
وانتقل المقبس من بيت الى بيت ، وجال في الحارة من أولها الى آخرها
نلح نرى كما كان دائما ، والسبيل وآكاها ، ومسجد البلدم ، ودمجع الجبر
والبقال والفرن نظراته مرلمه مع جد راس الحصد الكدنم والكبير ، وعلبت
كما شتى الحارة منزول القوة تأند النظرة . وارتفع صوت ارهضنة من وسط
الجمع أننا الدكام

ـ الزائر .. الدعاء الرحمي في الزائر في حضرة المنفش ..
فصاح شتى الحارة جذة غاضبا

ـ سكانة يا وليدة ..
وتوقع لتريده أنه تعليم المنفش وكأنه لم يفبه ، وبلا أنه بعومه ن لسعقب
آلر وأكول متى تكال شتى الحارة لسمرد بارض .. المقبس مع وشله
الدهماء م ؟
ولاحظ ذلك أيضا المعلم مصد الآدلاق مما حبه بيت الضرب ، والغناء ،
فأقتحم مع شتى الحارة أنه أخذه ان بيتم لسمرح في مجرة النا فورة
لبوث له شرابا باردا ، ورهذا يانما أن ستعلم شتى الحارة لراسم أتخاذا
لهم جميعا من الجرح.

ذهب المنفش الى بيت الآدلاق ، وراح الناس بيجاوردون ما سأتم
وتال رجل

ـ أراصد مع أسد المقبس بوشك على الكباء ..
تعال شتى الحارة كنه

ـ أنه أناس .. تول رأس قال العدوى ..
وتأمله من بيت الآدلاق نظرات الى الجمع نحو رافضة ، وطبل وتصنيس
وذلك شعوة من سبت فيال بيت الآدلاق وتأشمه دمعا

ـ أنه يرتعى .. من رأيضة لا يشبل له....
ورسم صوته وهو ينهي

نصيبك في الحياة لا ترم يصيب

واستمر ببها بدي يرقص ويغني

فتعاطف الناس مع جميع الركاب وأعدوا بيت الزلاقة

وألف الباكون مع النطاط بغنة !

وأعيد الجميع في الضحك ..

على فترة ما قضمت ، وسمعت ثاني لم أعرف في حياتي كلها حاربنا ، الفترة العا
عرفت ، الفترة السوداء . فترة غربة لم تمر حياتنا مثلها فيها نحمل ولا فينا نحرَّ ها
ولعل خير ما وصفت به حالة هذا النجم الأفول أن ذلك قد منح سبعة شبابيه . وهذا نسِ
يوماً لنا صمماً من واصل العمر والآخرة

ــ هذا الذي يجري تحت أعيننا ؟

فأجاب الرجل ونى

ــ والظاهر من الدخنة التي تمر بالنا سوتمرض وتموت مثل بقية المخلوقات .
والغريب أنه لم يعد ينام خوفا على أحد ، ولا يبيد أحدبجول سه الجمهور ، وسمتُ
ثم جيبتة الهاية تقول بـ فترة

ــ يبرى الفاسفين مرايا تنبذ وتمسَ ، وننشد العصمة وهم بيرتدة في مدنة
العالم .

وهكذا يوم نستلم نایلی ۱ دنبا وجرنا ، وکان وصنا ابعد صرصا ادکر ابنا ابن
الجيل . ذا يتی الدية نانم يبسم وجد ، أو هذا ما نصور ، هذا يتح جي سه ذكاته
وبيّع الخبرة من العبو هفة السماء وهو ير د لدى اب نا سا بقه

ــ لنا خليقة من القانون يعرف

ولم يتم خفير الدين وسهوس مع جميع راح أعمال الأزمية يبارد والشباح بلاد العلما
والامثال ، وحكايات السلف الصالح .

وبعد جاء بعرض المعلم ترسم الدولة فاشعل نار الغزل والفضول . كات يوم بالسوق
أو يوم السلب والنهب كلا يقولون ما ، وما هبت الأرض بالحرب والغزل والتقام .
وبقيتم نسيم البركة فيه هذه الصحارى وما بعد يتغير ساوّا

ــ وسع يا بني .. والعلم من المحافة

وجعل العبد ينت سه العلم صرخة مشقوبة . فارد الرجل الخوف يعني رفم كلوى وسع
انقاح نحو المردة . وصرح المبيع الوجيل وحلمه الى اقت ب دكاية ذ المعلم وقد
رسمت نياع الدم نفسيره ، وهذا يتمي الخارة وميلاد ، وجعل يحس العلم
فكبا عليه رصنا شال ، واستل ماغم الرحم وقال ــ

ــ خارجه السر الآلي ... هات المعلم برکة ..

في ملال الموت ، تلتذ الشيخ والرصبة بقم ا صباح يتبرمى على أ ملية العلم و
مخ يتمي الخارة ينظم ا الرحمه تعال كلو س سمبرت

وسم بقتّمت منه أحمد

فقال الرجل يشم

ــ يستمي الرحمة والنياية والضببارين

يكاد الجيب ما نعرف عند أنت الدولة المسلمين فني يدعم أصحاب الطلب ؟
أتوم آخره ما نفيد به ؟ ... ودار نرم لنترجل أن يريد معناه ... وقال ينتج الجارة
الدم يضطلع مد نويس ... وجعل القوى ليقاسم به تأيد نعيد ... لا نرى أن كيثريم نظام
نرده وعو تأبعو عنها ...
وتأخذهم بالدعاية الطفيفة اقبلوا أخرم عازلوا أحمد ... قال ينتج الجارة يقوم
- أما عارف أن نريد البركة لم يأتم عمها ...
تقال صوت
- تقلم وصوم نوقري الخمر وتأسفنا لتشيد الأبطال عنهم
وجمال دشتي حول ... ونتيح ... الخطأ عليه وكأنه بيثر عن ما بشير البرية ، وأما
شوال الوقت مبادل
- مد الذين نستخرج الخمر مد جبهة الخارج ؟ ... ولا ؟ ...
وبشر الجيب أنا بأمود عيدوى ؟ ويرتبش أن أعاد أصحاب النفوس سيادة وسيود ...
بأنهم يعمرونة في الطلبة والقانون ... بأبيع أصل النظام مد أبواب غطاء الناس
أن الحنفة تقوم أصل الغيب بتأسس مد الجيول ... تال ولى الله السيج رعاهم
- لم نشوا الخمر القديم
الناس لم يشرب معظم القديم الغام فود الخمر ، فقال السيج رعاهم
- ما مد أن الناس يخرج بما إلى الأقواس والخمر ، ... لم تجز القدرة مد أمال مباح
اعلم للدفاع مد هذا رضا البأ نشا ...
وشيع زبد وتردد مد أن لم يسد ، وأن أبام بسيمة الداية تولد أن أنت ، وهذا ٢٥٠
مد تولدوا مرة بنا ولد القوى - شتى نسيمه البرا- إلى الخمر ...
أعلم ينتج الجارة أن ربما يترب بعمد الجريمة فد أتخذوا مد الجسد القديم وكل ؟ فأنت
بيعمه رجال الآثار والثروة ود قلوا الجسد مد بابه وبعيسوا شكراه نظم
بعفوا إلى الدعاير والتأسيع ...
وأعلنوا ذلك بقوة ووضوح ، وحذروا الناس مد تصديم الترعات
وتبادلوا الناس النظر وتساءلوا متنكرين : أ يصدم هؤلاء الدعاية وأنكر ... ولى الله السيج رعاهم
وبأت الطبعة أن بيقة ٢٥٠٥

ـ تقف ثانية مرة الرسم ... في ... الخطبات ال... و...

ـ العربة ، عند السيل لفتت بعبده عيبنة الخ ، ملفتة شرائط ظلامه ..

ـ وأنا نجري وراء طريذ لك ..

ـ وأجتح ما ... ما بعمهم بمعنى نفذ السبيل نزهة ... ، ويأها بشئ الخارة نا قترب منك و صر نزل

ـ واستنفنوية البدء ومما يُرذ ؟ حقا ..

ـ فيما لت الحجوز با متقاصه

ـ له نرحم السنة السود

ـ كأنني نادلك يبقى بغير ترببه

ـ له نرحم الزلة وسوف نعرف نات يوم ناسة راه وأربه ..

ـ نزال الرحل ياسا

ـ ماذا تا لنرحم نعوذا لا نلهجيه وراك جديد لك ماضي له فيه ؟

ـ نعقف عننا المرة الناليثا وتمنا

ـ ... وكيف نغنى بعننا مس ماذا تا ؟

ـ تعال بشئ الخارة

ـ ... هو القدا باست فرحه

ـ نرننف الحوز

ـ وعبد رسم بعم

ـ وخدم الشيخ بشير ... النارية لبشى قليل ن البلد العلم نزا تم فرحة راحين

ـ نون بدور... ابه ترك حفيدها الدخه رسمت باشئ وذلك

ـ بشئ نبر .. هنا ظاقية مفيدا وخبرف عن مستقبل ..

ـ تعال الشئ

ـ لا دانني ونصال ك ابيه الناصرة وذلرابة الطيبة ، وذانا نهذا منك

ـ بأما باست فرحه

ـ وهم الظاقية ... رسم ببرو عد نزء الصبى تم نزال

ـ لا درسه الا عما ..

ـ غالت الحوز نبلس

ـ وذا بني صذا ؟

ـ لا درس الا عما .. ليس عندها أضيه ..

ـ ... هندك ولا تربد ديو تأسدى ..

ـ ابرا .. وتابك نترفم الفقر، وعليه بالصبر '

وصفت الجدة والحفيد وهي غير هنيّة

ونحول شيخي الجارة نحو الشيخ بشير قائلًا

ـ ماذا ؟ يخبرك لو سمعت على تعيب الناظر !

فقال له الشيخ :

ـ هذه قد تفسد وكأنها لا تأتب ، ولقد قلت للمرحوم والد

الصبي ركانة لم يبق كلامي نفع ... كما ...

محمد شيخ الجارة فيه بلاهة ... دنائك

ـ لماذا لم يردك ؟

فقال له الشيخ بشير :

ـ أنت تذكر لنفسها شاعر الرابط ذات أصيل بشباب وجمالها وهو يبني

ولعل الهوى فائق بعاجمهم

شد ما استقبله إلى برة بالساس ، وسرعان ما دعاه صاحب المعنى المغنّي

سيرائك ن صعوبة شاملة هزت جميع النفوس ..

هذه الرجل يبني وبارة تبسم وتفرّب حتى لدخ لي في عالمي الذي هو عالم

صغيري ، أنا نتطلّع من زينة المعلم يردي قادمًا وأمرّ صغت ضربة وقلت

له يد الصغير ستساعده على الرجاحة ، لم ينبه لقدري وحسبي ، سأله

إحسانًا فأعطاني بكرم المحود ..

فقال له شيخ الجارة :

ـ الم يزلك عما تقيمه ؟

ـ أبدًا .. ولا بدا معنا بذلك ..

ـ ولماذا لم تأخذ منه بما يحتّمه القدر ؟

ـ هذه لم نتجاوز الحدّ والله فضلنا اللغة !

ـ ثم ماذا ؟

ـ وإذا بهذرب الغيمة يبتغي ، وتتفمى مع ست بدرية هرم القاهر

بالباطل والذي تأكله لهنا في عاشر الأوّل ، وإذا بالبرة تنوّر

بلوا تقع ، ويبقى تهذينا الرقيع فاقد الحياة

ـ بدأ الغنّ عليها ثم قال شيخي الجارة

ـ قد نحوت المزة والرجل قبل ان يبق الحي للاستباء

ـ بشي ن غير الله

ـ وما معنى النجم الذي بعثت الحيرة عنه ؟

ـ انه يبقى ن معارفنا الحيرة والفهم والله أعلم .

عليه باطماً عنها ونشفت وانتشر السحاد . وكان الجو غائماً فى الاعتدال والوضاح .
وبدو ذاوية تالت الشخص جميعاً .. تلبي بندوى خوف نادر ".. وإذا هذا نفضف يتمل
الينا . وينم ذلا ينفع لذة نفسه . ونشيطه ولعبه وضحت ثم يأخذه الشدة
وبنيه بعد الشدة شدة حتى يجمد عنها أعير ويرتجب فى الاركان مرتبراً دد
اصماً كالعواء . وأكثر من صوت صياح
ــ الزم منزلك ورصنك
وتساقه انطلع فى الجو طوفانه من ريح تضاربه كتله الاتربة والرمال سوداء
ما تخضع لك كل شىء . ثارت الاتربة والاقمامى وكالقلائف من نزع الاسى . وصففت
الابواب والنوافذ . واختلط الصراخ بالبكاء . وتداخل النواء فى الصياح فى الوميم
وسمع فى وقيضه اشتد العنف وتعادى
وانطلقت الاصوات من بعا فلك
ــ اخ يهربم العصابة
ــ لم يجد العبيت فوه الرصد
صا صمر الشيطان ياشف مع عبابا ..
واستمر العنف كالمون حتى اسم المدعورين فى الظلاء نتيجة لا يبد فك . ومن
الانزعاج فعل يبنى الحارة وتلبه . حتى يضعم نفسه بانه يؤذى واجمع صياح بصوت
صناع فى العين
ــ اغلقوا الدكاكين .. اغلقوا الابواب والنوافذ .. لديهم احمد الخرير
وزوى اخ صعيد الزاوية . تجادل مع الامام لغته ماثرة . ونله احمد الامشيم
الى والزاوية
ــ هازا أنخاها على يا شيخ هارتنا ؟
نحا بنجوة غاضفة
ــ بنيت الفعل عندما تكتت العاصفة ..
ــ وكاننا لم نشهد منل ذلك من قبل
فضاح ؟
ــ بس سكول العد الرياح
واموا يتمطيوبو اعماقاً لتمره فاذا دمع غزيرة . واراد وجل بانيه
بت ذلك فى العيب نفى يبرت من محو من هلم آه وصى فى صيم اشفت
العاصفة وعادت فرنيف وبل بلغ من اليأس نفوة أنه دعونا منه الا علام قد فقد
التى الواقع فى حلم .
وتواصلت العاصفة فى العيب وقتل حتى ضيوط الليل . وذهبت كلا حيا وتبير

SAQI BOOKSHE/F

Saqi has been publishing innovative writers from the Middle East and beyond since 1983. Our new Saqi Bookshelf Series brings together a curated list of the most dazzling works from this kaleidoscopic region, from bold, original voices and contemporary bestsellers, to modern classics. Begin collecting your Saqi Bookshelf and discover the world around the corner.

For more reading recommendations, new books and discounts, join the conversation here:

🐦 @SaqiBooks
📷 @SaqiBooks
f Saqi Books

www.saqibooks.com

تمتد أحمد... بسم الله ... آوى ... بادر ... إلى الصوت الثقيل أنما يطفو على سطح
أسفله . وضى الطائر يعوضها السلامة و جعلت الصخور تطل من النوافذ والأركان.
وصمدت عند الإرادة شريدة عميقة طويلة اشتركت فيه جميع الصدور . وإذا سمرت
المدينة بريح تدفع مزيدها ما ضاع مناخ وعلمه العوصة " ... يصيب شي
الإرادة رصاح يعصينها

ــ التقى عند الناس وسيد الناس ما ترى
وتجمد الأصوات تواريت حمقوة بينهم الاستغاثة و صبر الحرب والذنب
والسليب ، مناعت الإموال وضاعت الأعراض.
وتابع شيخ الإرادة على الأصوات تعلم شديد
ويضت الأصوات تؤكد أن الصوص دخلوا من الحفر والقبور وهس عينا للتوزع
بعد ، وازدادوا عندا وضخونة حتى سدوا عين الشمس . وأنم انتهزوا دخمة
لهم في العاصفة في تيل أنفهم الذين أثاروها و يسعد عوضا من تصابك خيمه
ويصيل صديح ومرج دون أن شي ، لم تعد الإرادة تفزق بين السبعة وبين
وشيخ الإرادة
ويحمت قوة سمفلت نيام قطار عند باب الحصد القديم . تباركوا لله
والسد على الأبواب في الظلام و نغلعون هزب وينادمون إلى طلوع الفجر.